Puffin Books
Tales from the End Cottage

Mrs Apple lives in her cottage in Northamptonshire along with her pets: George and Shoosh the tabby cats, and Tooty, a very pretty Pekinese with royal connections. There are also hens in the hen field, and a horse called Browny and a dog called Rags who live at the farm next door.

They have a very peaceful life in the country and sometimes they think it might be a little too peaceful! But there's always something out of the ordinary happening, like bees swarming, or unexpected visitors turning up. And when Black Dog comes to the door seeking refuge, things will never be the same again!

This is a charming collection of stories full of the sights and smells of the countryside.

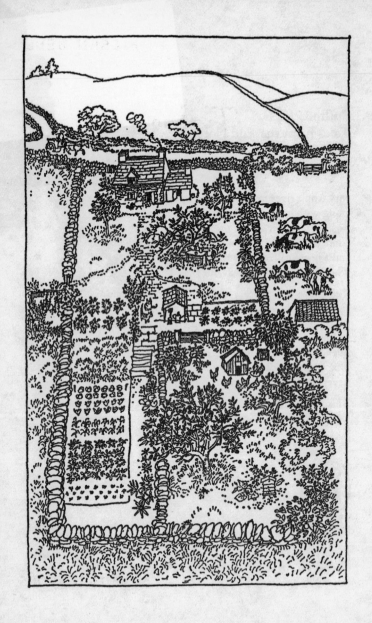

EILEEN BELL

Tales from the End Cottage

Illustrated by Prudence Seward

PUFFIN BOOKS

PUFFIN BOOKS

Published by the Penguin Group
Penguin Books Ltd, 27 Wrights Lane, London W8 5TZ, England
Penguin Books USA Inc., 375 Hudson Street, New York, New York 10014, USA
Penguin Books Australia Ltd, Ringwood, Victoria, Australia
Penguin Books Canada Ltd, 10 Alcorn Avenue, Toronto, Ontario, Canada M4V 3B2
Penguin Books (NZ) Ltd, 182–190 Wairau Road, Auckland 10, New Zealand

Penguin Books Ltd, Registered Offices: Harmondsworth, Middlesex, England

First published 1970
20 19 18 17 16 15 14 13 12

Printed in England by Clays Ltd, St Ives plc
Set in Linotype Pilgrim

Contents

I

Mrs Apple and her Animals

George Fat and Shoosh were brothers. They were large and beautiful cats with tabby coats. They lived together in

the country with Mrs Apple, and with Tooty. Tooty was a Chinese dog, a Pekinese, and very clever.

The cottage they lived in was built of stone, and there was a garden and an orchard. It was called the End Cottage, because it was at the end of the village.

Seven hens lived in the orchard.

Mrs Apple was very fond of her animals. She had a round smiling face and bright blue eyes.

The cottage was quite little. The way in was through a gate at the side, round to the back and up the garden path. This side faced the sun and was sheltered and warm. There were flat worn stones outside the door on which stood a bench, and often Mrs Apple's gardening boots. There was a holly tree and a damson tree.

The other side of the cottage faced the lane which led to the farm.

The door opened into a useful kind of room. At one end was the fire: at the other were the stairs which led up to two little bedrooms.

By the fireplace was Tooty's basket, where she slept. Mrs Apple slept in a feather bed upstairs. Her bedroom had white walls and patchwork curtains. Her red flannel dressing gown hung on a hook behind the door.

Sometimes the cats liked to sleep on her bed, but on fine summer nights they preferred to be out of doors. Shoosh stayed in the woodshed because he was fond of hunting, but George usually slept on a clump of thyme in the garden, because the moonlight shining on his fur made him feel very peaceful.

In the mornings when they woke up they went to look at the birds. The birds also looked at them. They did not really trust George and Shoosh, because they sometimes pounced.

After that the cats walked up the garden to say good morning to Mrs Apple and to Tooty. Then they asked for their breakfast.

'A little warm milk, if you please,' said Shoosh.

'Thank you,' said George, 'that is most delicious.'

One morning when they had finished their milk, Shoosh said that he would take a sunbath, and he lay down on the warm stones. George said he would go to visit the hens.

One of the hens, Mother Broody was her name, had been living in a little house of her own for some days. George visited her every now and then. On this morning she wasn't there, but inside the little house was a large straw nest, just the right size for a cat, and in the nest was a clutch of nice warm eggs.

'Cosy,' said George, stepping inside.

He curled round carefully, with most of the eggs underneath him, and settled down for a nap.

In a very short time Mother Broody came hurrying back. She was cross, and flew at George.

'Get off my eggs, my lovely eggs, you'll break every one of them, you clumsy great cat. Get off!' she shouted.

'My dear bird, keep your feathers on,' said George, blinking sleepily. 'What a to-do. There's nothing wrong with your eggs.'

He got up, and came out of the little house, stepping very carefully over them.

'Over-excitable, that's what's the matter with her,' he said to himself as he walked away under the apple trees.

Mother Broody scuffled and fussed and sat down with her back to him. It took her quite a while to arrange the eggs to her liking. All the same, George had kept them beautifully warm.

'I must thank him the next time I see him,' she said.

George went towards the strawberry bed. He met Tooty round the corner of the woodshed. She was lying on her tummy, catching beetles, and pretended not to see George.

George sat down and watched her for a time. Then he caught a small beetle under her nose.

'Not *quite* the way to behave,' said Tooty. 'You should

have asked me first whether you may catch my beetles. However, I don't really mind. I'm not very interested in beetles this morning,' and she walked away haughtily.

Shoosh came out from behind the wood-pile and helped George. They caught several more beetles.

'We won't mention this to Tooty,' said Shoosh. 'She mightn't be very pleased.'

'I'm hungry,' said George. 'Come on.' So together they went to find Mrs Apple. She and Tooty were sitting together outside the cottage door, enjoying the sun.

'Lunch-time,' she said when she saw the cats. 'Trust you cats to know that! Here you are,' and she put down two bowls of food. George and Shoosh ate out of one bowl, Tooty had a bowl of her own.

When they had finished Shoosh went indoors for his after-lunch nap, and George went to his clump of thyme. Tooty lay gracefully on the grass and sang a little song to herself. It went like this:

> *'I'm Madam Tooty-Pooty,*
> *I'm a very beautiful Chinese, . . . T C H A!'*

(this was a small sneeze to get the last bit of dinner out of her nose). Then, in a quick little gabble:

> *'I'm a sing-a-song of Pung Dog, Ming Dog, Ping Dog,*
> *Sing-a-song of Tooty-Pooty. – T C H A!'*

Then very softly as she fell asleep, 'Perhaps I'm the Emperor's *Aunt*.'

It was such a warm day that the animals rested quietly until tea-time, their favourite time of the day. They all joined Mrs Apple, and George purred most musically, while Shoosh asked for 'A little warm milk, if you please,' in his prettiest voice.

Mrs Apple held up a lump of sugar. 'Tooty,' she said, 'if

you want this piece of sugar you must ask for it properly. Are you ready? Bark in the right place. Now:

'If you want your lovely ...'

'*T C H A!*' said Tooty, (a sneezing kind of bark).

'You must say your ...'

'*WAH!*' barked Tooty, a splendid bark in exactly the right place. Then she sat holding the sugar in her teeth for a little while, to soften it before chewing it up.

After some conversation Mrs Apple said, 'Well, my dears, it's bed-time now.'

So George and Shoosh, who loved the evening and hadn't

the slightest intention of going to bed yet, disappeared like shadows into the bushes. But Tooty walked contentedly to her basket and curled herself up for the night.

2

Blackberries

One golden morning Mrs Apple got up early. She planned to go to the fields behind the cottage to pick black-berries, to make blackberry and apple jam. There were plenty of fallen apples down in the orchard, which she wanted to use up.

The cats watched her fetch the big enamel jug she always picked into. 'Shall we go too?' said George.

'I think not,' said Shoosh. 'We've got too much to do.' Indeed they had: the bees to look at, the hens to talk to, and, of course, the woodshed to look after.

Tooty went with Mrs Apple, trotting gaily along the lane with her tail well up over her back.

The old milk horse, Browny, was standing inside the gate of the backberry field. Mrs Apple gave him a sugar

lump which she happened to have in her pocket, and patted his neck.

'Good morning, good morning,' he said, rubbing his head against her. 'How nice to see friends. Beautiful day, after a beautiful night. Blackberries are ripe, and there are a few mushrooms – horse mushrooms you understand – if you look for them. Tooty, you and Mrs Apple follow me, I'll show you where to look.'

So off they went, with Browny leading the way. Tooty had to jump over the long grass, which was in places taller

than her head. However, by sitting up and begging now and then, she was able to keep Browny's haunches in view.

When they reached the hedge, Mrs Apple found plenty of berries. She had brought a crooked stick with her to hook down the ones which grew out of reach.

While she filled her jug, Tooty lay flat, with her tummy

on the cool grass. Her legs were short and the walk had used up a lot of energy.

Browny strolled down the hedge. By and by Tooty heard him make a pleased, snorting kind of noise. 'Come over here, my dear,' he called to her. 'Just turn that piece of grass back and look underneath it – and this one, and this one too.' Tooty went and did as he asked. There were

several fine mushrooms, their white tops glistening in the soft sunlight.

'What are you two up to?' asked Mrs Apple, coming over to them. 'Well! my goodness me, that's a good find. I'm very fond of mushrooms with a nice bit of bacon. Come along now, Tooty. Home, now. Browny, stand away from the gate while I open it. That's right. Good-bye.'

'Good-bye,' said Browny. 'It's been very nice to see you.'

'Good-bye Browny,' said Tooty. 'I like mushrooming. Will you call on us at the cottage soon? I hope so.'

When they reached home, Mrs Apple took her berries to the kitchen to weigh them, and Tooty went to look for the cats.

She found them sitting side by side, just behind the beehive.

'Those bees are up to no good,' Shoosh was saying, 'you mark my words.'

George put his ear close to the back of the hive. 'Sounds like purring to me,' he remarked.

'Bzzt!' said a bee, whizzing past George's nose. 'Zzt, Zzt!' several more followed it.

George withdrew his head hastily, and stepped back into the rhubarb. 'Funny sort of purring, that. Not like you and me. More excited than pleased, I'd say.'

'Here, let me listen,' said Shoosh.

There was a steady hum coming from the hive, because thousands of bees were all talking at once. This is what they were saying:

'Some of us will fly out, some of us will fly away and find a new hive. Too hot in here, no room to move, no room to buzz, buzz – want a new house – nowhere to put the honey – nowhere to put the honey – no room, no room, all the honey cells full up. Buzzzzz. We'll take the queen with us and find a bigger house. We'll swarm, that's what we'll do, swarm, swarm, swarm.' But because they were all talking at once George and Shoosh couldn't understand a word they were saying – nor could anyone else for that matter.

But the cats knew the habits of bees from experience.

'Those bees'll be out tomorrow, you mark my words,' said Shoosh again.

Tooty and the cats went back to the kitchen, where there was a most wonderful smell of blackberries and sugar being heated together. The wasps thought so too. They came flying into the kitchen in crowds, and made straight for the saucer where there was a little dab of jam put out to cool, for Mrs Apple to see if it had cooked enough to set. Mrs Apple flapped at them with a dish-cloth, and said, 'Get out of the way, you plaguey things.' This was no use at all. Wasps are determined creatures. They whizzed round her head, and back to the jam. 'Oh, well,' said Mrs Apple, 'live and let live,' and she rescued one with a spoon.

Just then a shadow fell across the window, and there was Browny's large gentle head pushing through.

Tooty barked with pleasure.

'Well, if it isn't the old horse,' said Mrs Apple. 'Here you are, I expect this is what you've come for,' and she handed him an apple.

'Apple from Apple. Ha! Ha!' said Browny, as he chewed it up. 'Thank you ma'am. Good Apple, good Apple!' and he went away chuckling.

3

Swarming Bees

The next morning everyone was very pleased to see that the jam had set. The pots were standing in a row on the window sill, with the sun shining through them, glowing with a fine dark red glow.

The mushrooms were sizzling in the pan, new bread was heating in the oven, and everything was nearly ready for a lovely breakfast.

At that moment George came trotting up the garden path.

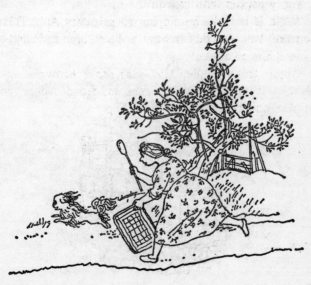

'Those bees *are* out,' he said. 'Shoosh is watching to see which way they swarm.'

Tooty jumped up and ran down the path barking, followed by Mrs Apple. Mrs Apple had picked up a tin tray which she beat vigorously with a wooden spoon as she ran. This is called 'ringing the bees', and country people sometimes do it to show that the bees which are swarming belong to them.

The noise was considerable.

When they reached Shoosh he twitched a whisker in the direction of the currant bushes. There were the bees, in a great cloud over one bush. The queen had settled on a branch, and they were beginning to cluster round her.

'That's good,' said Mrs Apple. 'When they've all settled I'll spray a drop of water on them. That'll make them cling the tighter to keep the queen dry. Then, come this evening, we'll put 'em back in the hive. But first, I must take some honey and give them some new comb. Then they won't want to come out again. They'll have plenty to

do, filling up the new comb, and plenty of room to do it in. That's what makes bees swarm – too much honey, and not enough room.'

Then they all went and had breakfast on the garden table, by the damson tree. Mrs Apple ate the mushrooms. The cats liked the hot bread with butter, but Tooty preferred it with jam.

When they had finished Mrs Apple said, 'I am going to spray those bees. You can come too if you like.' She went to the woodshed, and picked up a garden spray which she filled at the water butt. Then, followed by the cats, with Tooty at a safe distance behind, (after all, bees *do* sting), she went quietly up to the currant bush.

The bees were now in a solid mass, clinging round the queen. 'That will be all right to take,' said Mrs Apple. 'Now, a nice spray of water to make them hold on until I'm ready, and we'll have 'em in the skip in no time.' (A skip is a kind of straw basket used to hold a swarm of bees.) She squirted them gently.

'Silly things think it's raining,' said George.

Mrs Apple went back to the house to change into her bee clothes. She came out wearing Wellington boots, into

which she had tucked the legs of a pair of old trousers, but her skirt came down over the top so you couldn't really see this. She wore a jacket which had once belonged to a postman, buttoned up to her neck, and on her head a felt hat with a wide brim, and a veil which fell down round her face. She tucked the edges of the veil into the neck of the postman's coat. She looked very strange, but as she was going to take some of the honey store that the bees guard so carefully she had to be bee-proof, otherwise they would sting her to defend it.

The cats and Tooty had no bee dress, so they went to watch from a distance to be safely out of the way.

Mrs Apple went behind the beehive and gently lifted the roof off. Inside were the racks of honeycomb, full of honey. She lifted some out, put in some new racks, and

24

put the lid back on. She was so quick and quiet that the bees left in the hive hardly had time to buzz.

She carried the honey to the shed and shut it up inside to stop the bees fetching it back again.

Then she took off her bee dress and had a cup of tea, and waited a while before taking the swarm.

Just before dusk she put on her bee dress again. She took her skip and a sack from the shed, and followed by the cats and Tooty she went to the currant bush. The bees were quiet, and most of them were asleep. Mrs Apple held her skip under the clustered bees and gave the bush a sharp shake. Plonk! The whole cluster fell into the skip. She put the sack over the top before the surprised bees knew what was happening.

'That's the way to treat 'em,' said Shoosh approvingly.

Mrs Apple carried the skip full of bees to the hive. She made a sloping path up to the mouth of it with some planks, and spread a white sheet over it. 'Look, all of you,' she said. 'Watch them walk in.' She tipped up the skip, and the bees came tumbling out on to the sheet. Surprised but sleepy they sorted themselves out, and got to their feet.

'Come along, come along,' said their leaders. 'This way in. Here's our home,' and in they all marched, looking like black treacle flowing uphill.

It was almost dark by the time the last bee was in the hive. Mrs Apple yawned. 'Come, Tooty,' she said. 'I'm sleepy. Bed-time.' And she picked Tooty up in her arms. 'Come, cats, bed,' she said. But there wasn't a cat to be seen, except perhaps the flick of a tail disappearing into the shadows.

4

The Visitor

One day Mrs Apple had a letter from her friend in the town. The letter said: 'Can Rex come to you next Wednesday? I want to go to see my sister for the day and I can't take him with me because she doesn't like dogs, and I don't like to leave him alone from breakfast until supper. I would put him on the bus, if you could meet it. He is an intelligent dog, and would be quite all right.'

So Mrs Apple called all the animals to tell them.

'Will Rex come in the cottage with us?' asked Tooty. 'I don't believe my plate holds enough for two – especially

if Rex is a large dog. Not that I'm greedy, of course, but one must eat. And another thing, I won't let him get into my basket.'

'Gently, gently, my dear,' said Mrs Apple. 'Don't run on so fast. We can make arrangements for all these things.'

The cats had been sitting a little apart. George was dozing, and Shoosh was doing his whiskers, so they did not seem to be listening.

'I could do with some help with the rats,' said Shoosh, 'so he can come to the woodshed with me. I shall be on top of the corn bin, in case he is unreliable about cats.'

'He could eat out of our dish — after we've finished with it, of course,' said George. So it was all settled.

When Wednesday came the animals all got ready to greet Rex. The cats still felt a little uncertain, so George sat on the stone wall behind the flower border and Shoosh went up the damson tree.

'You never know with dogs,' said George, and Shoosh said, 'You can't be too careful.'

Mrs Apple brushed Tooty and tied a red bow round her neck. Then she went to meet the bus. It arrived just as she reached the bus stop.

'Here's the dog, Mrs Apple,' said the conductor. 'Been very good all the way. No trouble at all. More sense than some humans I won't mention.'

'Thank you so much for looking after him,' replied Mrs Apple. 'He'll be coming back with you on the evening bus. Come along, Rex, come and meet my animals.'

When the visitor came in at the garden gate the animals saw a large shaggy honey-coloured dog.

'What did I say?' said Shoosh, going further up the tree. George said nothing, but he got quietly off the wall – on the field side.

Tooty rushed to her basket and said as loudly and as quickly as possible: 'I'm a sing-a-ping-a-Mung Dog, Sing Dog, Sung Dog, and you can't touch me in my basket, you horrible hairy great thing. And what is more, if you do I shall *scream*.'

'Be quiet, Toots. That's no way to behave. Remember your manners,' said Mrs Apple. So Tooty began to make growly noises instead.

'Come here, Rex, come and meet Tooty,' said Mrs Apple, putting her hand on Rex's collar.

Tooty looked as if she might be going to burst. As Rex drew near her growls became growlier, and her red bow quivered. She began again, in a high squeaky voice. 'I'm a sing-a-song of Sung Dog, Ping Dog – *Be off*, I say: MY basket!'

'Pardon me, Madam,' said Rex in a dignified voice, 'I have no wish to intrude in any way. However, it *is* considered polite to say good morning to one's hostess, and that is what I am doing.'

Then Tooty felt ashamed of herself. She rose in her basket and said in a shaky voice, 'Forgive me, sir, I was overcome by your size. Welcome to our humble home. All I have is yours.'

'Goodness me, Toots,' said Mrs Apple. 'Whatever is the matter with you? Stop being so affected, and talk properly. Now, Rex, off you go; go and look at the garden, and make friends with the cats.'

So Rex bounded out of the cottage door. 'Hello, you cats,' he barked. 'How's hunting in these parts?'

'Quiet, you dog,' said Shoosh, coming part of the way down the damson tree. 'If you make such a fuss there won't be a rat to be seen for weeks.'

Rex said he was sorry. 'Must be the excitement you know. Not used to travelling.' Shoosh flicked his tail as a sign that he understood.

The top of George's face showed over the wall, as he peeped at Rex. Then the rest of him appeared as he slid

cautiously over the wall and into the flower bed, where he lay watching.

Rex ran off down the garden, so George came out of the flower bed and Shoosh came down the tree.

'I think I'll try him on those rats,' said Shoosh.

'Rather you than me,' said George. 'I shall keep my distance for a bit longer. He's a very big dog.' They went down the garden together, and then George took the path to the orchard, while Shoosh went to the wood-shed.

Rex was sniffing about the floor and discovering rat holes. He found the smells so interesting that he took no notice of Shoosh. Shoosh walked past him and jumped on top of the corn bin. They spent the rest of the morning hunting, and when Mrs Apple called everybody to luncheon they walked up the path side by side. Rex had straw and grains of corn stuck to his coat. They were

looking pleased with themselves, and appeared very good
friends. Later, Mrs Apple found five rats' tails lying on the
floor of the woodshed.

Tooty got out of her basket and sat beside Mrs Apple,
and George came in quietly, asking for his milk. They were
both still rather shy of Rex.

When lunch was over, Mrs Apple tidied the cottage and
had a rest in her chair. Then she called all the animals.
'Come along,' she said, 'we'll go to the orchard and feed
the hens.'

Mother Broody had taken her children to live in the
orchard with the other hens. She fluffed out her feathers
when she saw Rex. 'Now be careful please,' she said. 'My

children are young and tender, and not to be frightened,'
and she spread out her wings to protect them.

'I wouldn't dream of touching them, Ma'am,' said Rex.
'I have seen chicks before, in the market town where I
live. They pack them in boxes there, without their mother,
and sell them for a shilling each. Very sad.'

'Poor little things,' said Mother Broody. 'It's dreadful to
think of chicks without a mother,' and a tear gathered in
the corner of her eye. She cuddled her babies under her,
and one climbed on her back and snuggled down between
her wings.

The rest of the hens were scratching about for worms,
chatting as they did so. Mrs Apple threw corn to them.
Then she came to Mother Broody and scattered corn for
her. She put food for the chicks on a flat dish. They were
too young to eat corn, so they had crumbled hard boiled
egg, with the curd from sour milk.

'I'm going indoors now, to make some scones,' said Mrs
Apple. 'So you animals must look after yourselves.'

'Would you like to walk down the lane to see the cows,
Rex?' asked Tooty. She felt less shy now, because Rex had
been gentle about the chicks, and she wanted to make up
for being rude to him that morning.

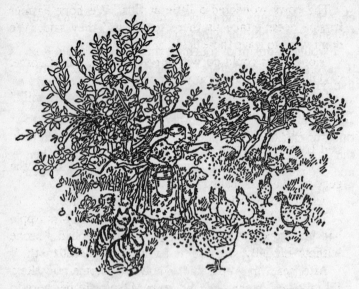

'Oh, a walk!' barked Rex, bounding towards the gate. 'A walk! That is exactly what I should like,' and away he galloped.

'I shan't go as fast as that,' said Tooty. 'My legs aren't long enough.' She stretched, kicked with her back legs, sneezed, 'TCHA!' and trotted off after him, her tail well up over her back.

Rex was waiting for her in the lane, and she showed him the way to the field where the cows lived. The cats went too, but they jumped over the wall and followed the path through the fields, and they all arrived at the field together.

The cows came and put their noses under the gate and blew gently at Rex. 'Pleased to meet you,' they said.

Rex told them about the market town where he lived, ten miles away, and how farmers bought and sold their animals there on Thursdays.

The cows wondered a little at this. 'We hope Farmer Parsloe doesn't take us there to sell us,' they said. 'We don't want to leave these fields.'

'None of us could do without your milk,' said George. 'So I don't think there is any fear of that.'

'Ah, no,' said a big brown cow. 'We give lovely milk.' And 'Lovely milk,' they all mooed together.

'Let's go home now, and see if those scones are cooked,' said Tooty. 'Good-bye, cows.'

When they reached the cottage they could smell the good smell of well baked scones.

'Come along,' said Mrs Apple. 'Tea is quite ready.'

Tooty had her sugar lump in a saucer of tea, Mrs Apple had hot scones with damson jelly, and Rex had a scone without the jelly, because he hadn't got a sweet tooth.

After tea, Mrs Apple said, 'Time to go home now, Rex. I'll take you to the bus, and your Missus will be there to meet it in the town.'

So Rex said, 'Good-bye, and thank you for a lovely time,' to Mrs Apple, and 'Good-bye, good hunting, you chaps,' to the cats, and 'Good-bye, Madam, delighted to have met you,' to Tooty, and the visit was over.

5

Baking Day

There were little scratching noises outside, and two pussy voices were saying: 'MEE-OW; MEE-OW! oh MEE-OW! Please be quick and let us in. We're two hungry cats this morning.'

'Come along in,' said Mrs Apple, opening the door. 'You want your breakfast, do you?'

George and Shoosh rubbed against her legs, purring. 'Good morning,' they said. 'Chilly, this morning. Have you noticed? If it gets colder we'd like to sleep on your bed.'

Mrs Apple poured milk into their bowl, and added a dash of water from the kettle singing on the hob. 'Warm milk, this morning,' she said. 'Autumn is on the way. There's quite a nip in the air, and the leaves are blowing off the damson tree. Up you get, Toots, come out and feed the hens, then we'll make some bread.'

Tooty jumped out of her basket and ran to the door.

'Hear that, Shoosh?' said George. 'Bread making. The kitchen is the place for us today.'

Tooty and Mrs Apple went through the garden to the woodshed. The wind was gusty, and the holly tree rattled its leaves as they went past. Tooty's tail blew out behind her in feathery streamers. Mrs Apple filled a tin pannikin with corn for the hens. A mouse who was having breakfast behind the corn bin scuttled into his hole.

The hens came running to the gate of the orchard when they heard Mrs Apple and Tooty coming. 'Tchook-tchook-tchook!' cackled a long-legged white hen, running faster than the others. 'Here's breakfast! Eat up! Eat as much as you can! Keep the cold out!' and she jumped up and tried to reach the corn in the pannikin before Mrs Apple had scattered it.

'Now, you greedy, just you wait your turn,' said Mrs Apple, throwing handfuls amongst them. All the hens began pecking and scratching in the grass for the grains, pecking at each other occasionally as they did so.

Mrs Apple looked about her. 'I should like to get those apples picked today, before the wind gets them,' she said.

37

'I might do that whilst the dough is rising. Come along, Toots, back we go.' She put the pannikin back in the wood-shed, and picked up a few logs for the fire.

Back in the kitchen, Mrs Apple shut the window. 'No draughts,' she said. 'Cold airs and cold hands can ruin a batch of bread.' She took her apron from the hook behind the scullery door. It was made of faded blue cotton, gathered at the waist, and tied well behind, with wide frills round the armholes. Then she washed her hands and warmed them by the fire.

Tooty, curled in her basket, watched with interest. She was very fond of the little crispy bits which fall off bread at baking time.

Mrs Apple scooped five scoopfuls of flour from the flour bin into her largest mixing bowl, and sprinkled it with salt. Then she set it on the hearth to warm.

The flour bin was made of wood, shaped like a little barrel but wider at the bottom. It was kept on a stool beside the fire. The salt box hung on a hook above it. It too was made of wood, with a flap lid fastened on with a strip of leather for a hinge. Both were shiny with use and age.

Next, she fetched the yeast from a jar on the pantry shelf, and crumbled it into a blue and white flowered mug. 'Mrs Watson, at the shop, said the baker got it fresh yesterday,' she said approvingly. She covered the crumbled yeast with sugar, and put the mug on a shelf above the oven to get warm. She put lard and hot water in a jug, and stirred it about. Then she added cold milk and tested it with her finger. 'Just warm to my finger. That's right,' she said. Next she fetched baking tins, floured them, and put them on the shelf to warm.

Then she sat down by the fire to wait. Tooty dozed in her basket. The cats purred and the clock ticked. The kitchen had become very warm. Mrs Apple roused herself. The warmth made her quite sleepy. 'I wonder if the yeast is ready yet?' she said, and looked in the mug. Interesting things had been happening. The yeast and sugar had melted together, and the mug was filled with a creamy froth. Mrs Apple stirred it, and a warm and pungent smell filled the kitchen. Tooty opened one eye and her whiskers twitched. 'Lovely,' said Mrs Apple. 'All ready for mixing.'

She rolled up her sleeves, made a hollow in the flour with her hand, and poured in the lardy milk and all the yeasty froth. Then she plunged both hands in and began to mix.

She mixed and kneaded, mixed and kneaded, until the bowl and her hands were both quite clean, and the dough lay in a soft lump. She slapped it gently to one side, floured

39

it, and slapped it back again. Then she covered it, bowl and all, with a clean cloth, and put it up by the baking tins. 'Sit there awhile, and rise,' she said. 'Come, Tooty. We'll go outside and cool off a bit. I see the sun is shining.'

They slipped through the door, which Mrs Apple shut carefully behind them. She sat down on the bench and spread her hands on her knees. They felt pleasantly soft and smooth from the dough. Tooty lay full length on the stones and rolled. Mrs Apple lifted her face to the sun and shut her eyes. 'Make the most of this whilst it lasts,' she thought.

Mr Blackbird sang in the damson tree. Then the sun went in and it began to get chilly. The gate clicked, and Mrs Apple opened her eyes. Farmer Parsloe came round the end of the cottage, his dog, Rags, at his heels. He carried a basket full of logs on his back.

'Reckon you'll soon be needing these,' he said. 'Grows

chilly mornings and evenings.' And he went down the path to the woodshed.

Tooty got up and sniffed noses with Rags. They were old friends and pleased to see each other, so their tails were wagging.

'Hello,' said Tooty. 'How are the cows?'

'Nicely, thank you,' said Rags. 'We're bringing them in from the fields tonight. Farmer Parsloe thinks there may be a frost. It'll be warmer for them in the cow house.'

'We're making bread,' said Tooty. 'I'm waiting for it to be cooked. I like the crispy bits.'

'Bread isn't much in my line,' said Rags. 'Bones are what I like,' and the two animals lay side by side, chatting.

Farmer Parsloe finished stacking the logs in the wood-shed and came and sat down on the bench.

'Some of those logs are apple,' he said. 'Burn slow, smell sweet. Talking of apples, have you picked all yours yet? I could do with a bushel or two of Bramleys for keeping.'

'That was something I was going to do today,' replied Mrs Apple. 'There are still a few left on the tree. You can have them for the picking, and welcome. I'll show you,' and they went down the path to the orchard.

'Let's go and talk to Browny,' said Tooty to Rags. They found him waiting with the cart in the lane. He was cropping the grass on the verge.

'Hello, my dear,' he said to Tooty, looking up with his mouth full. 'No more mushrooms and blackberries this year, I fear. These cold nights will finish them off. I sleep in my stable now.' He went on eating. The dogs lay on the grass listening to the gentle sounds of Browny tearing off tufts of grass, and munching them.

Mrs Apple and Farmer Parsloe came out through the cottage gate, carrying the log basket filled with apples.

'You've been some time,' remarked Browny. 'Ah! Lots of apples, I see. Ha! Ha!'

'Here you are, you soft old thing,' said Mrs Apple, offering him a lump of sugar. Browny pushed his nose into her hand and nuzzled it as he took the sugar. Then he chewed it up with loud scrunching noises.

'These apples'll do nicely. Thank you kindly,' said Farmer Parsloe, climbing into the cart. 'Come along, Rags. Gee up, Browny.'

'Thank you for the logs,' said Mrs Apple, turning to go

back to the cottage. Farmer Parsloe waved his hand, and Browny trotted away down the lane.

The dough had risen up to three times its size, and filled the bowl completely. Mrs Apple put on her apron and began to shape the loaves. She pulled off a piece of dough, folded it over itself, and put it into one of the tins. She did this with all the dough. Then she put the tins back on to the warm shelf. 'Rest there and recover,' she said.

She opened the oven door and tested the heat. Then she made up the fire, wiped the table, and put the bowl, the jug and the mug in the sink. Then she looked at the loaves. The dough had started to rise again, so she popped all the tins into the oven.

'There we are, Tooty,' she said. 'Now all we have to do is to wait while it bakes. I'm going to have a nap while it does it.' She sat down in the armchair and put her feet on the fender. Tooty lay on the rug beside her.

Soon the kitchen was filled with the delicious smell of baking bread. When it was ready Mrs Apple lifted the tins from the oven, tipping out each loaf in turn. As she tipped out each loaf, she tapped it underneath to see if it was done.

Plenty of crispy bits fell on the floor, and Tooty gobbled them up.

By tea-time the bread was cool and ready to eat, and with butter and blackberry jam it tasted very good indeed.

6

The Arrival of Black Dog

One chilly morning with a nip of frost in the air, Mrs Apple said to her animals, 'I'm going to market today. I shall buy dog biscuits and fish, and candles and custard powder, and some red pepper to put in the hens' mash, to warm them up a bit.' So she put on her coat, tied a scarf

over her head, took her basket from the hook behind the door, and set off to catch the bus at the end of the lane.

Tooty settled down in her basket beside the fire and George and Shoosh went upstairs to curl up together on Mrs Apple's bed.

The fire burned brightly and the cottage was very quiet.

By and by a small scratching sound broke the silence. Tooty lifted her head and looked over the side of her basket. The door moved a tiny little bit. There was a

45

louder and more determined SCRATCH! SCRATCH!
The door swung open, and in walked a fine black Peke!

Tooty was astounded! She could hardly believe her
eyes. She thought she was the only Peke for ten miles
around. And here in the cottage kitchen was this fine
animal. He had a beautiful glossy coat and flashing black
eyes. He carried a bundle tied up in a red spotty handkerchief.

'Anyone at home?' he called, then, 'Oh good, a lovely
fire.' He tossed his bundle into a corner, and sat down on
the hearthrug to warm his back.

'Hello, my dear,' he said, noticing Tooty. 'Nice place
you've got here,' and he curled up and went to sleep.

Tooty was so surprised that she just sat and stared at

him. Then she got very quietly out of her basket, crept
close and sniffed at his fur. It smelt of fields and frosty

46

weather. Black Dog sighed luxuriously in his sleep and stretched his legs. Tooty crept quietly back to her basket and lay with her chin on the edge, watching him. 'He is a splendid animal,' she said to herself. 'I believe I might give him some of my dinner when he wakes up.'

Just then he did wake up. He walked over to her basket and said, 'Move over a bit, lady, there's a draught out here,' and got in.

Tooty was affronted. Even from another Peke, she would not put up with that. She hopped out the other side as quickly as she could, and began to sing her cross-dog song, which goes like this: 'I'm a sing-a-song of Ping Dog, Sung Dog ... M Y basket! Go away you great bully, or I'll *bite*!' Then she lay down by the fire and sulked. Black Dog took no notice at all. He stayed in the basket and went to sleep again.

Tooty found that it was not very amusing to sit and sulk with nobody taking any notice. What is more, there *was* a draught. So she got up and edged her way into the bit of basket that wasn't full of Black Dog, and lay looking at the fire and at the red spotty bundle in the corner.

Soon there were two soft thumps on the floor above, as the cats jumped off Mrs Apple's bed. They came walking down the stairs. 'I'm a bit peckish,' George was saying, 'I wonder where Mrs App . . .' Then he saw Black Dog. 'Blackbirds and Bats!' he hissed. 'Just look at that heap of black fur in Tooty's basket!' and he leapt on to the top of the chest of drawers.

'Can't have that sort of thing. I'm going to turn it out,' said Shoosh, and he rushed towards the Pekes.

'He's a Ping Dog, Ming Dog. Wha! Tcha! ...' Tooty began to bark – but she got no further, because Black

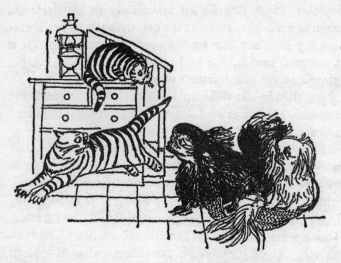

Dog leapt from the basket, and before you could say 'Tails
and whiskers' he had chased Shoosh out of the door and
up to the top of the holly tree. Black Dog sat glaring up at
him from below.

'My dear sir,' said Shoosh, when he had got his breath
back. 'There is no need to behave with such violence. If I
had realized your Pekeness I would never have done such a
thing. A heap of black fur was all that I saw – could have
been anything.'

'A heap of black fur indeed,' growled Black Dog. 'Use
your eyes and wits, my dear Cat,' and he glared up the
tree.

George and Tooty came out of the cottage. Tooty said,
'Black Dog, splendid animal as you undoubtedly are, you
must stop this, and allow Shoosh to come down from the
holly tree. Here, we are peaceful people . . . And, *it is MY
basket*. Please remember that.'

48

George simply said 'Lunch-time,' and walked indoors.

Shoosh came down from the tree, and they all gathered in the kitchen to see what Mrs Apple had left for them.

On Tooty's dish there were small crisp biscuits and little pieces of raw meat. In the cats' bowl there was fish, and

some brown bread to make up. There were two saucers, one containing milk, the other water.

'This works out all right,' said George. 'Two and two, that makes four. So Shoosh and me one bowl. Tooty and Black Dog, t'other bowl.'

Tooty was about to protest that her bowl only contained a helping for one person, whereas the cats' bowl . . . but she was glad she had not because Black Dog dragged his bundle from the corner, untied it and spread out the contents. In it were a slice of brown bread, a dead mouse, and two pieces of sugar.

'Here you are, Cats,' he said, tossing the mouse towards them. 'More in your line than mine. And here, dear lady, this is for you. I expect you have a sweet tooth to go with your pretty face. I shall eat the bread myself, I am used to a low diet,' and he passed Tooty the two sugar lumps.

She was quite overcome. 'Oh Black Dog,' she said, 'have some of my meat to go with your bread, and we will have a piece of sugar each. I will teach you my happy song to sing after you have eaten it.'

After that the cats offered some of their fish, so it ended in everyone eating out of both bowls and sitting by the fire to finish off the mouse and the sugar.

Then Tooty sang her happy song. It goes like this:

> *'Half a pound of twopenny cheese,*
> *Half a pound of treacle.*
> *That's what makes a Pekydog sneeze, (Tcha!)*
> *Wauf! goes the Weasel.'*

Black Dog learnt it very quickly and they sang it together, getting softer and softer, until they fell asleep on the hearthrug. They lay there all the afternoon.

When they woke up there was a wispy mist rising from the fields. The old milk horse Browny trotted past the window. 'Clip-clop, clip-clop,' they heard him say. 'Bless me, I can hear my feet but I can't see 'em.'

By and by the cottage door opened, and Mrs Apple came

in. The cats rubbed round her legs, and Tooty said 'Wuff.'

Black Dog lifted his chin from the hearthrug, and looked up at her doubtfully. Mrs Apple bent down. 'Well I never,' she said. 'Who have we here? Is he a friend of yours, Tooty?'

'He's a Ping Dog, Pung Dog. YES. I like him very much. He brought sugar. MY basket,' said Tooty, all in one breath, and jumped into it.

Mrs Apple patted Black Dog and sat down by the fire to take her boots off.

'We must find out who you belong to,' she said to him. 'They'll be wanting you back.'

The cats climbed on to her lap, and Black Dog lay with his chin on one of the discarded boots, while Mrs Apple warmed her toes. They all had tea. Then Black Dog got on to her knee with the cats.

The next day Mrs Apple asked all round the village if

anyone knew of anyone who had lost a Peke. Nobody did. So she put up a notice in Mrs Watson's shop. It said:

FOUND
A fine Black Peke. Anyone who has lost same, apply:
Apple, End Cottage (up the street).

But nobody came, so Black Dog settled in, and lived happily ever after with Mrs Apple and her animals.

7

Black Dog's Story

The weather had turned cold and wet. The lane was nearly impassable, a sea of mud, and the deep cart ruts were filled with water.

The cats picked their way down the garden path, shaking their feet and twitching their fur. When they arrived at the woodshed they were usually in a very bad temper. The straw on the floor was wet, but there was still a little comfort to be had on the logs piled at the back, and up on the rafters. It was a dull time for cats, as most of the rats and mice slept all day.

Tooty and Black Dog hated mud. When they got it on their fur they just dried off by the fire, and then lay on their backs waiting for Mrs Apple to comb their feathery feet and their tummies.

Mrs Apple plodded about in a pair of Wellington boots, feeding the hens and bringing in Brussels sprouts, saying, 'Oh deary me, never did I see such mud and nasty weather. I shall never get the washing dry.'

The hens stood about in dismal groups, their shoulders hunched and their feathers stuck together by the rain, quirking and grumbling. It was a trying time of the year for everybody.

Inside, the cottage was warm and dry, the kettle sang on the hob and the firelight shone on the bright red curtains.

One evening, after tea, the animals were lying on the

53

rug by the fire, while Mrs Apple did her mending. The rug seemed hardly large enough for four animals and Mrs Apple's slippered feet – at least, not if everyone was to get the warmth of the fire in the right place, and there was plenty of shoving and grumbling.

At last, Black Dog jumped on to Mrs Apple's knee. 'Stop it, you lot,' he said. 'You don't know when you're well off.

Do you know where I spent the last lot of bad weather? You don't, so I'll tell you.

'I started life as a town dog. My mother lived in a basement room, in a great big town, a long way from here. That is where I was born, one of a litter of three pups.

'There was no garden, and all the sunshine we saw shone down a flight of steps, which led up to a noisy street. Motors rushed past, and people walked by all the time. You couldn't put your nose outside without getting stepped on.

'My mother and sisters liked this, called it "seeing life", and they enjoyed the gossip with the neighbours. I didn't. My coat became rough and dull, and worse still, I didn't relish my meals.

'Then one day, a woman and a little boy came to the door, selling clothes pegs. My dears! The smell of their boots! Glorious! Well, being country animals, you all know that smell, of earth and grass and sweet air. She had another smell about her, delicious and exciting, the smell of woodsmoke. Well, she bent down, and I sniffed at her hand, and she pulled my ears in the way that I like. "I'm coming with you," I said, and when she left I trotted close to her heels. Her skirt was long and full, and no one noticed me follow them on to a bus.

'After a few stops they both stood up so I jumped off before them, and stood waiting. The conductor shouted to the woman as she stepped off, "I didn't say you could bring that dog on here."

' "I ain't got no dog," she said. Then she saw me. "Well,

I'll be blowed. How did you get there? You'd better buzz off home now, or they'll say I pinched you."

'Just then, the small boy picked me up, *most* uncomfortably, round my tummy. I longed to nip him, but I controlled myself, and turned round and licked his cheek. Well, the woman took no more notice. The child caught hold of her skirt with one hand, and, nearly strangling me with the other, set off with his mother across a patch of waste ground towards a caravan. This was painted green

and yellow, and had a chimney with smoke coming out of it. There was a horse hobbled a few yards off, more children, and a man and a big boy.

'No one spoke when we arrived. The child carrying me took me inside, and sat down with me on a bunk. I curled up behind him, and pretended to be asleep.

' "They'll say yer pinched that dog," said the man. "Did you?"

' "No," said the woman. "He just followed. No time to take him back. Anyways, Jem likes him. Let him stay, he's quiet."

'So I settled down with the gipsies. We had a lovely summer, travelling about, stopping the caravan on the wide grass verges of lanes. We went from village to village, with clothes pegs and lace to sell, and enjoyed the sun and summer weather.

'The gipsies made rabbit stew, in a big black iron pot, over the wood fire. When food was plentiful we all shared it. My fur became thick and glossy. Jem wasn't too bad, and I made friends with the horse. I used to sleep out near where he was hobbled at night. "Fine in this weather," he said. "But you wait, my boy! You wait!" – and my goodness, he was right. The days got shorter – dark soon after six o'clock, and cold, and wet. That was the worst: wet grass, wet kindling so that the fire wouldn't burn to cook the stew. Nowhere dry to sleep. The gipsies hated it too.

'This year they decided to go to the camp. "We'd best be getting to winter quarters," they said. "Can't take that dog, Jem. He'll fend for hisself."

' "You'd better go," said the horse. "Too many of us in winter quarters, and food is scarce. You'd be better off on your own."

'Jem gave me the sugar, and the horse gave me some bread. I tied them up in a red spotty handkerchief, and set off. I caught a mouse myself, and put it in too. I'd been walking all night when I got here. That's why I was a bit sleepy. There's no place like a cottage fireside in the winter – or a cottage garden in the summer. Take my word for it, because I KNOW.' Black Dog gave a sigh, and snuggled close into Mrs Apple's lap.

'Oh, purrrr, purrrr,' said the cats. 'He's right, you know.'

8

Mrs Apple has Toothache

One cold winter morning Mrs Apple came downstairs looking pale and tired. 'I've been awake all night with the toothache,' she said. 'I must catch the bus to go to the dentist and ask him to make it better.'

The Pekes were very sympathetic. 'We will look after the house,' said Black Dog.

'Wrap up well. It's very cold,' said Tooty.

Mrs Apple gave the Pekes their breakfasts and fed the hens. She put down saucers of bread and milk for the cats.

Then she put on her big thick coat and tied her head up in a woolly scarf.

'I'll catch the early bus back,' she said. 'I should be home by four o'clock,' and she set off down the lane to the bus stop.

The cats came in from the woodshed. 'I wonder if there's anything for lunch?' said George, bread and milk all over his whiskers.

'Never known an animal so interested in its tummy,' commented Black Dog. 'Won't hurt you to miss a meal, my cat.'

'Mrs Apple will be back in time for an early tea,' said Tooty. 'She forgot about luncheon because her face hurt.'

'We'll go and hunt,' said Shoosh. 'Come on George,' and off they went.

Black Dog and Tooty settled down by the fire. Presently they began to doze. This is a good way of spending a cold morning when you are looking after a cottage.

It was very quiet. Out of doors the trees dripped with moisture, mist hanging in their branches. A robin sang a little song in the holly tree. Farmer Parsloe and his dog, Rags, passed by in the lane, on their way to fetch Browny from his field. 'Too cold to leave the old horse out this weather,' said Farmer Parsloe. 'Besides, I may need him if the mist should come down thick.'

Soon the Pekes heard him coming past again. This time they could also hear the clip-clopping of Browny's shoes.

'End Cottage,' said Browny. 'This is where we stop for apples. Ha! Ha!' He stopped outside the window, chuckling. Farmer Parsloe pushed it open.

'Anyone in?' he asked. 'Hello. Two Pekes keeping house. Has Mrs Apple gone on the bus? Nasty day for her to be

out. The mist is getting thicker. I'll look in later, to see if she's back.'

'No apples,' said Browny sadly. 'Bad, that.' Farmer Parsloe shut the window again. 'Gee-up,' he said, and Browny went clip-clopping away to the farm.

'Toots,' said Black Dog by and by, 'I'm hungry. Let's see if we can find anything to eat.'

They hunted about in the kitchen. It seemed quite bare. 'But I do think I can smell biscuits,' said Tooty, lifting up

her nose and sniffing. Black Dog jumped on a chair and put his paws on the window sill.

'Oh good,' he said. 'You're right, Toots. Two ginger biscuits. One each. Here you are,' and he dropped one at her feet.

Then, each carrying a biscuit, they went back to the fire.

They ate them on the hearthrug.

Then they sat and looked at the fire. They were still hungry.

It began to get dark and the fire was nearly out.

'Let's go and meet the bus,' said Black Dog. 'It must be coming soon.' So the two Pekes, feeling rather subdued, trotted to the bus stop outside Mrs Watson's shop.

They sat down, close together, to wait. Moisture hung on their whiskers, and they shivered a little.

Presently they heard a horse and cart coming. 'I think that is Browny,' said Tooty.

The horse stopped on the other side of the lane. 'Whoa! Wait, Browny,' said Farmer Parsloe's voice, and Farmer

Parsloe's large figure showed for a minute against the light as he went into Mrs Watson's shop. He couldn't see the Pekes huddled together in the foggy dusk.

'Where is this bus? Time it came,' said Black Dog. As he spoke the door of the shop opened, and Mrs Watson's voice said, 'I don't believe Mr Watson will bring the bus back in this weather, Farmer Parsloe. The mist hangs very thick in the lanes.'

Farmer Parsloe came out and shut the door. He crossed the road and climbed up into the cart. The Pekes heard him say, 'Gee up, Browny,' and the sound of Browny's hooves died away in the distance. There was silence.

'Oh, Black Dog,' said Tooty. 'Whatever shall we do? Do you think Mrs Apple won't come back tonight?' and she began to whimper in a little squeaky voice.

Black Dog wasn't feeling very cheerful himself. His thick coat was soaked through and sticking to him.

'Never mind, Tooty,' he said. 'We'll wait a little longer because if the bus does come Mrs Apple will need us to guide her home. Humans can't find their way in a fog as well as animals can. Snuggle closer against me, and we'll both be warmer.'

So the Pekes sat huddled together in the chilly dark.

Suddenly Black Dog jumped up. 'Toots,' he barked. 'The hens! They aren't shut in, and it is just the night for the fox to come!' and putting his nose to the ground, he ran for home. Tooty followed at his heels. They ran through the garden and squeezed under the gate of the orchard.

'Where are those cats?' panted Black Dog. 'Cats! Cats!' he called.

'Uproarrrrr. Uproarrrrr,' said a fat purring voice close at hand, and George's face appeared out of the mist.

'You've frightened away all the rats,' said Shoosh huffily, coming out from under the hen cub.

'Never mind the rats,' said Black Dog. 'Have you seen the fox?'

'Oh, him,' said Shoosh. 'Haven't seen him. Can't eat foxes.'

'Oh, Cat, use your wits,' said Black Dog, exasperated. 'Foxes EAT HENS. Mrs Apple isn't here to shut the trap door to keep the fox out, so we must do it for her. Come, Tooty,' and he and Tooty ran to the door of the cub.

All the hens were inside, miserable and chilly. 'Never known anything like it,' they grumbled. 'Nasty evening like this – no tea – not shut in. Where's Mrs Apple? Where's everybody? Haven't seen a soul since this morning. Heard those cats hunting about, but they didn't come in. Busy with their own affairs. No time for us. A shame, really. Too bad. No tea. Nasty day. Move *up*, Mother Broody, that's my perch. Yes it is. Always has been – well, it is now, anyway. You can sit on those eggs. No one seems to want them. No one's been near us all day. Too bad. Too . . . GOODNESS! what's that? Keep still everybody. Quiet!'

They stopped talking and crouched quite still, listening to Black Dog and Tooty coming to shut the trap door.

'Wuff,' said Black Dog pushing his head inside their little door. 'Wuff. Wuff. Here we are, hens. We'll look after you. Up on your perches, and make room for Mother Broody. We're going to shut your door to keep you safe from the fox.'

'Oh dear Black Dog,' said Mother Broody, 'how kind of you to come. What has become of Mrs Apple?'

So Black Dog explained about the bus not being able to see its way in the fog.

'Now,' he said. 'We must get this thing shut. Help me, Toots.'

The doorway that the hens went in and out by was a square hole just the right size for a hen. The trap door that Black Dog wanted to shut was made to slide up and down over this hole. When it was open it was held up by a ring on a chain, the ring hitched over a nail.

By standing on the tips of his back toes Black Dog was able to reach the nail. He struggled, and bumped his nose. But the ring stayed where it was.

'Oh, dear,' he said. 'That doesn't make it come off.'

'Black Dog,' said Tooty, 'I have an idea. I'll push the trap up a little further by putting my back under it. Then the chain will be slack. That will make it easier to slip it off the ring, I think.'

'You clever Peke,' said Black Dog. 'We'll try.'

So Tooty put her head in through the little door and wriggled her way in. Some of the silliest hens began to giggle and say: 'Goodness me. Whatever next? A dog in a hen cub! Whoever saw the like of that?' and they

pecked in the direction of Tooty. But Mother Broody said, 'Be quiet, you stupids. Can't you see what our clever Pekes are trying to do? Keep out of the way, and be quiet.'

Tooty put her chin on her front paws and lifted up her hind quarters, taking the weight of the trap door on her back, near her tail.

'Fine,' said Black Dog, 'that makes it easier. I'll put my paw against the trap, so that it won't come down and squash you! Now!' He struggled with all his might to get the ring off – and succeeded.

Tooty wriggled out. Black Dog let go of the trap, which

came down with a sharp BANG. 'Good night, hens,' called both Pekes. 'You're all right now. Sleep well.'

They could hear the hens settling down, already sounding sleepy, saying 'Good night. Good night. Move up, do. MY bit of perch. You'll fall off if you push. CLUCK! I told you so.'

The cats came out from behind the hen cub. 'Let's all be in the house together,' said George. 'Warmer than in the woodshed. Then we'll all be there if Mrs Apple does get back.'

So they made their way through the garden, under the dripping trees. Inside the cottage it was quite dark, and the fire was out. It was not comfortable, and it was not cheerful.

'There is one thing about humans,' said Shoosh, 'they can make fire and light. No animal can do that.'

'I *like* humans,' said Black Dog. 'And I wish one was here now.' He lay down on the hearthrug, his nose on his paws. Tooty lay beside him. A tear trickled down her nose.

'Come upstairs to Mrs Apple's bed,' said George to Shoosh, and they went. But the Pekes lay watching the door.

Some time later, Tooty pricked up her ears. 'What's that, Black Dog? Do you hear anything?'

Black Dog's head was up. He was listening hard. A tiny sound was in the air. A very faint rumble of wheels and a far away 'clip-clop'. The Pekes strained their ears to hear. Was it coming closer? Could it be Browny? Yes! Clip-clop, rumble-rumble, clip-clop. CLIP! It stopped outside.

Farmer Parsloe's voice said, 'Here we are, Mrs Apple. Safely home again. Well done, Browny.'

Mrs Apple's voice said, 'I do thank you, Farmer Parsloe, for bringing me back. Browny is much better than a bus in the fog. Bring him up in the morning for sugar and apples. I'm thankful to be home to my animals. OH! The hens!' she cried. 'They aren't shut in! The fox might come,' and she came hurrying through the gate.

The Pekes jumped up and rushed to meet her.

'I'll see about the hens,' said Farmer Parsloe. 'You get in out of the cold,' and he disappeared down the garden.

The Pekes went wild with joy. They jumped round Mrs Apple and barked. Black Dog ran and brought one of her shoes to her.

'Goodness me, what a welcome,' she said. 'Did you think I wasn't coming back? You must be nearly starved, my poor dears. Never mind. We'll soon have the fire going and get the tea.'

Mrs Apple lit the lamp.

The cats came downstairs yawning. 'I always knew she'd get back,' said George. 'Purrrr, Purrrr.'

Soon the fire was burning brightly, and the kettle singing. Mrs Apple put four dishes of food by the hearth. Then she made the tea.

Farmer Parsloe put his head round the door. 'You've got good neighbours,' he said. 'Those hens were shut up.'

Black Dog lifted his face from his dish and winked at Tooty. 'There are some things that humans *don't* know,' he said.

9

Christmas

Christmas was coming. All the animals knew it, but they didn't know just *when*.

'We shall know when the time comes,' said George. 'We always do.'

It was going to be Black Dog's first Christmas at the cottage, and they were all very excited.

Mrs Apple had made the puddings and tidied up the house. She was ready to go out and pick the holly when the right moment arrived.

One morning Tooty said, 'I think it's nearly here. I feel it in my furry toes.'

'My word, you need furry toes this weather,' said Black Dog. His coat was bushy and black, and he had frost on the ends of his whiskers.

'Always is cold here, when it's Christmas,' said George. 'We'll go out to the fields tonight. Then we'll know.'

They watched Mrs Apple make a garland of ivy and hang it over the fireplace. That afternoon she went to the holly tree and picked a bunch of crackly leaves and bright red berries. She made it into another garland and hung it over the cottage door. Then she went to sit by the fire to wait for Christmas morning.

The cats went quietly over the hard ground. Their feet made a tiny crunchy sound and left paw-prints in the frozen grass.

Tooty and Black Dog murmured, 'Just like Peking,' to each other as they trotted along the path to the field.

Browny, the horse, was there waiting for them. They all stood looking up at the sky. The moon was riding high, a small pale globe. The stars glittered in the frosty air. It was completely still, and very, very cold. So still that they could hear the quiet breathing of the cows in the shed, over by the hedge.

'This is Christmas,' whispered George.

The holly tree stood with all its leaves glistening and its berries glowing. Quite still, and quite, quite silent.

'This is Christmas,' whispered Shoosh. 'Listen.' And across the fields they heard a distant bell ringing, a sign to all who heard.

All the animals jumped up.

'Christmas!' they called. 'Christmas! Merry Christmas!' and ran to Mrs Apple.

'Merry Christmas, my dears!' she said. 'Browny, mind your head on the lintel.'

'Christmas comes but once a year. Apple please, Mrs Apple. Ha! Ha!' said Browny.

The Pekes chased each other upstairs through the bedrooms, and down again. The cats purred and rubbed on Mrs Apple's legs. Browny scrunched apples and said, 'Ha! Ha!'

'Sleep time now,' said Mrs Apple. 'Off to bed all of you.'

The cats and Browny went out to the sheds. The Pekes went to Tooty's basket, and Mrs Apple went to her feather bed.

The stars and the moon shone brightly, the holly tree glistened in the moonlight. Everything was happy and quiet. It was Christmas.

Snow

One morning after Christmas, Mrs Apple looked out of her window and saw the whole world outside under a white blanket of snow. Snow lay thick on the grass. The branches of the trees had a coating of it sticking to one side where the wind had driven it, and it had frozen on.

'Those cats will never get up the path in this,' said Mrs Apple. 'And I shall have a job getting to the hens. I must go and see to things as soon as I've lit the fire and had a cup of tea.' So she put on her red flannel dressing gown and blue felt slippers and went downstairs.

There was still a bit of red in the fire, the logs hadn't quite burnt away. With a handful of dry twigs and a knob or two of coal she soon made it burn up. 'Lucky I brought in water last night,' she thought as she put the kettle on. 'The well top will be frozen on, I shouldn't wonder.' She went upstairs to dress while the kettle boiled.

When she came down the Pekes were awake. 'Grufph,' said Black Dog getting out of his basket and trotting to the door. 'Whatever is this interesting kind of nothing smell?'

'Oh Black Dog,' said Tooty. 'I know, it's SNOW. Lovely, lovely stuff to roll in. Our great-grandfathers had it in Peking. But it's horrid when it freezes in lumps on the fur of your tummy.'

'Wait a minute, Pekes,' said Mrs Apple. 'Let me finish my tea, and I'll take you out. Too much snow against the door to open it yet. We don't want all that messy stuff inside.'

She drank her tea, put down the cup, and picked up the coal shovel. When she opened the door the snow was like a little wall with a sloping top where it had built up against it: shiny and icy. Mrs Apple shovelled energetically while the Pekes pranced, impatiently. When she had cleared it away, 'Off you go, dogs!' she said, and the Pekes rushed

out – and sank up to their tummies in snow. But they bounded and barked 'Beautiful! Wonderful – Oh, my furry feet, what fun!' and Black Dog bit a big lump of it, just because he felt so happy.

'The cats are not going to like this,' said Mrs Apple. 'Come along you Pekes, see where George and Shoosh are.' They made their way through the snow, to the woodshed.

Mrs Apple opened the door. 'Meeow! Oh Meeow!' wailed George and Shoosh, crouching together on the rafters. 'O meeow, no mice, no rats, beastly draught, and SNOW. We hate this. If we'd know it was going to snow we'd have stayed in the cottage all night! Oh MEEOW!'

'Come along you silly pussies,' said Mrs Apple. 'Come down off that, and come in to breakfast. Then I must go and see the hens.' So George and Shoosh came down gingerly, shaking their feet and complaining. They made such a fuss that Mrs Apple picked them up, one under each arm, and marched up the path to the house with them.

The cottage was warm and comfortable. Firelight was shining on the walls, and on the bright rag hearthrug. There was a strange white reflection on the ceiling. 'Snow light,' said Mrs Apple. There was a big pan of potato peelings boiling on the hob.

Breakfast was porridge for Mrs Apple, warm bread and milk for the cats, and biscuits with a little lean bacon for the Pekes.

When they had finished Mrs Apple took the pan of peelings off the hob, strained the water down the sink, and put in handfuls of hen meal, which she kept in a bin under the sink – one handful for each hen, and one for luck. She mixed it all up. A warm, brown, mealy scent filled the kitchen. The cats' whiskers twitched, and the Pekes lifted their noses in the air, snuffling with pleasure. Mrs Apple added a sprinkling of red pepper. 'Warm them up a bit,' she said, taking a shawl from a hook behind the door. She wrapped the shawl around her, picked up the pan of steaming hen mash, and set off down the path to the hens' field. The Pekes followed her, but the cats said, 'Not this morning, thank you,' and went upstairs to Mrs Apple's bed, where they curled up in one round lump for the rest of the day.

The Pekes ran on ahead of Mrs Apple. When they reached the gate there was not a sound from the hens' cub.

'What's going on?' said Black Dog. 'This doesn't seem right. Why aren't they talking?' and he pushed his way under the gate. He ran quickly towards the cub, his nose close to the ground.

'Phuff, phuff,' he said. 'I know that smell. Phuff. Where is he?' and he ran round the cub to the fence belonging to the field where the cows live. 'Phuff, phuff! This won't do. *Where* is he? I must find him. Phuff Phuff!' and he ran down beside the fence. Then suddenly he saw the fox, all ginger-bright fur and sharp nose, with his teeth showing, crouching in the ditch.

'Be quiet, you!' said the fox. 'Be quiet, and don't see me. Then, when old Apple's gone, we'll round up these silly hens, and have a great feast.'

'The very idea!' shouted Black Dog, and barked and barked. '*Me* rounding up the hens? *Me*! the trusted guardian of Mother Broody and her children! You scurrilous animal –' and he rushed at the fox with his head down, as if to butt him in the tummy. The fox drew back and snarled, but he dodged away from Black Dog's charge, and made a grab at him. He missed. Mrs Apple and Tooty came running up.

'What is it, Black Dog? What have you there? Oh! My goodness! The FOX!' and Mrs Apple threw the hen meal pan at him. Such a muddle! Meal pan, Black Dog and fox, all in a heap together.

Fox said, 'No place for me,' and cleared the fence with a bound. Black Dog, who had a certain amount of hen meal in his fur, shook himself.

'Brave and *clever* dog,' said Mrs Apple. 'Come and see if the hens are all right.'

In the cub, all the hens were clucking away, saying,

'He's gone now, my dear, it's all right. Black Dog was too much for him. He won't come back. Cluck! Cluck! That's *my* egg, Mother Broody. No, *mine*. Get off! Cluck! Cluck!'

'They're all right,' said Mrs Apple. 'Just hear them prating. Here's your mash, you silly dears, not much of it spilt. Have it in the cub, now. You'd best stay indoors while it's so cold.'

When the hens had finished, Mrs Apple and the Pekes went back to the cottage, Tooty trotting beside Black Dog, proud to be the friend of such a gallant animal.

A little snow goes a long way, so the Pekes spent the rest of the day by the fire, while Mrs Apple did the ironing.

II

Good-bye, Winter

Mrs Apple woke in her feather bed before the sun was up. She sat up in bed and looked out at the new day. Clear, whistling trills floated in through the window. 'That's Jinny Wren singing,' said Mrs Apple to herself. Mr Blackbird said 'Plook, Plook,' in a loud but sleepy voice, and a cascade of lovely notes floated down from the top of the damson tree. Mrs Apple jumped out of bed and looked out of the window.

'Ah! the thrush,' she said. 'He hasn't sung like that since last spring – he knows winter is going.' She dressed quickly and went downstairs.

The Pekes were waiting, yawning and stretching, at the bottom of the stairs. Mrs Apple opened the door. The air was soft and warm. 'Lovely,' she said, and breathed deeply. Tooty rolled on the grass, paws waving. Black Dog kicked with his back legs, and lifted up his voice and barked loudly.

'That's an awful noise to make,' said George, looking down from a branch of the holly tree. 'Can't you shut up and let me do my bird-watching in peace?'

Black Dog took no notice. He rushed round the corner of the cottage and dashed out of the gate, growling and barking at Rags, who was going past in the lane. Rags growled back, and they walked round each other on very stiff legs. Tooty came running. 'Black Dog,' she called, 'stop it! You can't fly out at Rags like that. He's on his way to help Farmer Parsloe with the cows. Stop it at once and beg his pardon.'

'Dear, dear,' said Black Dog. 'A mistake, it seems.' He stopped growling, and so did Rags. 'Forgot you're a friend

of the family. Beg pardon, and all that. Farm dogs aren't friendly to gipsies, and I got into the habit of getting my bite in first. No offence taken, I hope?'

'Not fond of gipsies myself,' said Rags. 'But it can't be too pleasant to be on the wrong end of the bite, so to speak. I quite understand. No offence taken where none intended.' They both wagged their tails, and Rags went on his way.

Tooty and Black Dog went back into the garden. 'We haven't seen Shoosh this morning,' remarked Tooty. 'I expect he's in the woodshed. Let's go and look.'

Squeakings and thumpings were coming from the wood-shed. George had left his bird-watching and was crouched beside the corn bin, his cheeks puffed out, his whiskers pricked. As the Pekes arrived there was a particularly loud thump, and Shoosh leapt over the side of the bin, a mouse in his mouth. He leapt almost on top of George. 'Get out of my way,' he spat, very cross. 'M Y mouse,' and he clumped George over the head with his paw. George hissed and hit him back. Shoosh dropped his mouse, and in no time at all they were rolling all over the floor, spitting, hissing and yowling most horribly, and kicking each other with their back feet.

Tooty was terribly shocked. 'Oh pussies, pussies!' she cried. '*Please* don't do that. You'll hurt each other.'

Black Dog rushed at them, barking his loudest. 'Stop it! Stop it this minute, I say!' he shouted, jumping up and down with excitement.

The mouse ran a little way, and turned round to watch. Then it popped down its hole.

At this moment Mrs Apple arrived. 'Goodness gracious me,' she said. 'Whatever is going on here?' and she flapped at the kicking ball of fur with a sack. The cats went on fighting, so Mrs Apple dropped the sack on top of them. A cat shot out from each side, and disappeared from sight. The sack lay still on the floor.

'I should think so, indeed,' said Mrs Apple. 'And if any of you want any breakfast, come at once,' she added, and walked away up the garden. The Pekes followed her.

Shoosh came out from behind the corn bin and began to wash his tummy. George came down from the rafters and walked to the door and looked out at the garden. 'Fine morning for the time of year,' he remarked. 'How about a little breakfast?'

'An excellent idea,' replied Shoosh, and they walked up the path side by side, their tails waving.

After breakfast Mrs Apple said, 'I shall go to the farm now to fetch some milk. You can all come with me if you like.' The Pekes were delighted, but the cats decided to stay at home.

Mrs Apple picked up her milk can. It was made of shiny tin, with a lid, and a handle you could swing it by when it wasn't full of milk. They set off towards the farm.

Mrs Apple dawdled down the lane. The hedges were bare and brown, misty-looking in their branches. Tom-tits swung upside down singing their shrill little song. The earth at the foot of the hedge was bright with tiny new leaves of violets and primroses, ivy and baby cow-parsley, and of all the plants which would soon make a tangle of leaves and flowers.

The Pekes trotted along happily, sometimes dabbling their feet in the runnels of water that flowed at the edge of the path, or snuffling delightful smells at the foot of the hedge, causing blackbirds to fly out, chip-chipping loudly. Once Black Dog jumped into the ditch in which ran a small gurgling stream, drained from the fields. It was cold, and he jumped out again, quickly.

Flocks of little birds, chaffinches and yellow hammers, were feeding on the plough-land, and a big flock of pigeons rose from behind the hedge with a great clapping of wings.

They turned in at the farm gate. Farmer Parsloe was in the cow house, cleaning out after the morning's milking. 'Good morning,' he said. 'Lovely, isn't it. Can you wait a minute whilst I finish? Then I'll get your milk.'

So Mrs Apple went round to the sunny side of the building, and sat down with her back against its stone wall.

The Pekes lay beside her. All around them was bright green grass, and even brighter green mosses grew amongst the stones. There were celandines, and one small pale primrose.

'Look, dears, there's a rabbit,' said Mrs Apple very quietly. It was close by, lying on its side by the entrance to its burrow, enjoying the sun, like everybody else. It was a very young rabbit, and its fur glinted with a silvery sheen.

Black Dog opened one eye and looked at it. Being fond of young animals, he had no wish to chase it. 'Rabbit in the sun. Rabbit in the stew. Very nice,' he murmured.

Tooty looked at him with drowsy admiration. 'Oh, Black Dog,' she said. 'What a thinker you are.'

Farmer Parsloe came round the corner of the cow house

carrying the milk can. 'Here you are,' he said. 'Straight from the morning's milking, just cooled a little. You'll find it nice and creamy. The cows are enjoying the fresh grass.'

So Mrs Apple took her can, and she and the Pekes walked home, quietly content, the sun warming their backs.

12

The Gipsies

Tooty and Black Dog were helping Mrs Apple to make an apple pie, from the very last Bramleys, stored all winter. The fire burned brightly, the oven was hot, and the apples were peeled. Mrs Apple rolled out her pastry to the proper size for her pie dish. Then she cut the apples into thin slices, filled the pie dish with them, and added sugar and four cloves and a dash of water.

Tooty sat at Mrs Apple's feet, waiting for the moment when she trimmed the pastry lid of the pie. Little pieces of pastry always fell on the floor for her to gobble up. Black Dog was under the table chewing apple skins. An odd thing for a dog to like, but Pekes are special dogs.

Footsteps sounded outside on the garden path. Tooty looked up. 'Visitors,' she said. 'Who can this be? I don't know those footsteps.'

'I do,' said Black Dog, and bolted underneath the armchair, where he was completely hidden by the frill round the edges of its seat. There was a knock at the cottage door. Black Dog growled softly. 'What's the matter, Black Dog?' asked Mrs Apple, popping her pie into the oven on her way to open the door.

On the doorstep stood a gipsy woman and a little boy with a dirty face. Black Dog stopped growling, and lay still.

'Good morning lady,' said the gipsy to Mrs Apple. 'You've got a kind face, lady. Buy my lucky lace, lady. Bound to bring you luck,' and she took a hank of rather grubby lace from her basket.

'No,' said Mrs Apple. 'I don't want lace. I'd never use the stuff. But I don't mind buying some willow clothes pegs. I had some when you came last year. How have you been getting on, since you were here last?'

'Oh, cruel hard, it's been,' said the gipsy. 'We had to get rid of a dawg. Black, 'e were, with great big eyes ...'

Suddenly Tooty understood. These were the gipsies that Black Dog had been with, before they turned him off and he came to live at End Cottage.

'NO!' she barked. 'He's *not* coming back to live with you. He's my friend. He lives here.' She began to sing her furious song. 'Sing-singa-Ping Dog. YAC! YAC! Scarra, scarra! WAH! *BE OFF* I say!'

Jem, the boy with the dirty face, got behind the gipsy

woman and aimed a kick at Tooty with a large and heavy boot.

'Don't you dare do that –' began Mrs Apple. She was interrupted by a hurtling lump of black fur. It was Black Dog.

'*I* saw you, you beastly little boy,' he growled. 'You leave her alone, and GET OUT OF THIS GARDEN.'

'Pekes, Pekes,' cried Mrs Apple. 'Whatever is the matter? I've never heard such a fuss.'

'That's my dog,' said Jem.

'Rubbish,' said Mrs Apple. 'He has lived here for months. Turned up last autumn. Starved, he was, too.'

'That's my dog,' said Jem again, and he grabbed Black Dog by the thick fur at the back of his neck, and started to walk towards the gate.

Tooty rushed after them, screaming as she ran: 'Put him down, you beastly little boy! Put him down, I say.' She tried to grab hold of Jem's heel. He kicked her off, and went through the gate into the lane. Tooty burst into tears and ran to Mrs Apple.

Mrs Apple was very cross indeed. 'You tell your little boy to put that dog down,' she said. 'I never saw such goings on. That dog's been here months. He's not a gipsy dog. Come here, Toots.' She took Tooty in her arms and followed Jem out of the gate.

Outside in the lane stood the gipsies' caravan. It looked nice, with its green paint and yellow trimmings, the lace curtains on its windows, and the jolly-looking iron chimney sticking up over the roof. Black Dog's old friend the horse was peacefully cropping the grass at the edge of the lane. Smoke was coming out of the chimney, and there was a smell of rabbit stew. Underneath the caravan hung buckets, and a bag of onions, also a coop with four hens in it. Their heads were sticking out between the bars of the coop to see what was going on.

'What have they been up to now?' asked a brown hen. 'Dog stealing, do you think? Looks like it to me. As if they hadn't enough dogs. That spotted one is already one too many, I say,' and she looked towards a large animal lying close to the coop, under the caravan. The dog looked at the hens, lifted its lip, and snarled.

Jem came through the gate, dragging Black Dog by the neck. The door at the back of the caravan opened, and a man put his head out. 'What you got there?' he demanded. 'Oh him again.' He seized Black Dog, thrust him inside the caravan, and shut the door.

Mrs Apple, Tooty and the gipsy woman arrived on the scene just as the door banged.

'Where's my dog?' demanded Mrs Apple. 'Just you undo that door and give him back to me this minute.'

'He's our dog, lady,' said the man gipsy, leering. 'If you want him I'll sell him to you for five shillings.'

'The very idea,' said Mrs Apple. 'Buy my own dog! Just you let him out of there, and give him back.'

Tooty whimpered in Mrs Apple's arms. Black Dog, inside the caravan, barked and barked.

'Shut up, you,' shouted the man gipsy, and banged on the door. 'Or you'll get a taste of my boot.' Black Dog went on barking, and the man hammered on the door again.

Mrs Apple was beginning to wonder what to do next, when along the lane came Rags, Farmer Parsloe's dog, on his way to fetch the cows. He walked over to see what was going on.

'Whatever is all the row about?' he asked, coming closer to the caravan.

'Rags! They've got Black Dog shut up in there, and –' began Tooty, when 'Yawk!' said Rags very loudly. 'Ah! you beastly cur, nip me, would you. Come on out of there, and fight properly in the open. Come on out, I say!' He tried to get at the gipsy dog, which had snapped at the back of his leg, from underneath the caravan.

All he could reach was its ear which he caught hold of in his teeth.

'Oh sir!' yelled the gipsy dog. 'I didn't mean no harm. What's a snap more or less? I only did it to defend these dear hens. I'm only a poor dog. I don't mean no harm. Leggo my ear, kind sir.'

'Just listen,' said the hens. 'Did you hear that? Cluck! Cluck! "Dear hens", indeed. When you remember that only yesterday he tried to eat Maria. Half the feathers gone from her tail. Such a liar, that dog. Don't you believe a word he says.'

Rags let go of the gipsy dog's ear and came towards Mrs Apple and Tooty. The gipsy man aimed a kick at him, and at the same instant the spotted dog rushed from under

the caravan and bowled him over in the lane. Then the fight really began. Rags was underneath lying on his back, doing his best, but getting rather the worst of it. Tooty struggled out of Mrs Apple's arms and rushed screaming to his aid. She could do nothing but scream, but she did that very well. Black Dog in the caravan was nearly frantic, and could be heard rushing up and down smashing things, and barking. All the humans were shouting at the same time. 'Call your dog off,' Mrs Apple shouted, and, 'Tooty, come here.' The gipsy woman yelled 'Jem. Jem. Stop that dog in there breaking things, or I'll tan the hide off of yer.'

The gipsy man just swore, but, like Tooty, he did his part very well. The horse, who was used to a rough life, went on grazing as if nothing was happening.

Into this turmoil walked Farmer Parsloe. He swung his stick. The gipsy dog rushed for shelter under the caravan, and Rags rose to his feet, very out of breath, and bleeding a little from one ear.

'We said never believe a word he says,' cackled the hens. 'Poor dog, indeed. He's nothing but a coward and a liar, and his master is just as bad.'

'What's going on?' asked Farmer Parsloe.

'Oh, give them five shillings,' said Mrs Apple. 'I can't stand no more of this. They've got Black Dog shut up in there and won't let him out until they are paid five shillings. They say he is their dog. Well, we don't know where he came from. But do give them five shillings and make them go away.'

S M A S H! sounded from inside the caravan.

'I think you'd better open that door if you want any crockery left,' said Farmer Parsloe to the gipsy man. The gipsy looked very surly, but the woman slipped behind him and opened the door.

What a sight met their eyes! There stood Black Dog in the middle of a most tremendous muddle, with everything in the caravan upset round him. Farmer Parsloe looked at Mrs Apple and grinned.

A large vase lay smashed with all the paper roses that had been in it scattered on the floor. There was broken china everywhere. Pictures were hanging crookedly on the walls. The big SMASH that they had heard was the rabbit stew being knocked off the stove. Most of it was on the floor, but some of it was in the bed. Black Dog was on the bed too, shaking the insides out of a pillow he had just ripped open, and the air was thick with feathers.

'Blimey,' said the gipsy woman reverently. 'What a bloomin' awful mess!'

Black Dog stepped carefully over the bits of broken china, and joined his friends in the lane, while everyone gazed at the wreckage.

Farmer Parsloe looked. Silently he handed five shillings to the man gipsy, who took it equally silently.

The spotted dog dashed between their legs into the caravan, and began to eat rabbit stew.

The gipsy woman went inside, and shut the door. The man gipsy went to the horse's head, jerked it up from the grass, and started to lead it up the lane.

The caravan door opened and the spotted dog hurtled out. Jem and the spotted dog followed the caravan as it went on its way.

'I don't think they'll try that trick again in a hurry,' said

Farmer Parsloe. 'Certainly not where Black Dog is concerned. But they only got what they deserved.'

'Isn't lunch a little late?' asked George, coming through the gate. 'Has something been happening?'

'Pah! Cats!' said Rags, shaking a sprinkling of blood over everyone.

'Goodness, that ear!' said Mrs Apple. 'Bring him into the cottage and let me wash it. Will you stay and have some apple pie?' She brought a basin of water and bathed Rags' ear.

'Thank you kindly,' said Farmer Parsloe. 'But I must be getting along. All right now, Rags? Come along then,' and Farmer Parsloe and Rags went on their way to the fields.

The two happy Pekes ran into the cottage, where everything seemed cosier than ever after such an eventful morning.

'I'll never let that gipsy inside my gate again,' said Mrs Apple as she shut the door behind them.

13

The Pullets Leave Home

The sun shone, the blackthorn was in flower, and Mrs Apple was busy every day in her garden. She dug the earth and raked it smooth. She pruned the roses and tied back the clematis. Every now and then big black clouds rolled up and down came showers of rain and hail.

'In like a lamb, out like a lion,' said Mrs Apple, in March. Then, as the days went by, 'April showers bring forth May flowers,' she said, as she dashed for the shelter of the woodshed, an old sack flung over her head to keep the rain off.

She sowed her vegetable seeds in neat, straight rows: carrots and turnips, lettuces and spinach.

'You ought to try this,' said George, rolling luxuriously on the seed bed, rubbing his furry side on the warm earth.

'Get off there, you dratted cat,' said Mrs Apple unsympathetically. 'Never did I see such bad gardeners as cats. How can the carrots grow if you roll all over the rows?' But she wasn't really cross. The spring made her happy too. 'We'll soon hear the cuckoo if this keeps up,' she said.

The animals could feel spring in their bodies. They lay stretched in sunny sheltered places and their fur became shinier.

The hedges were covered with tiny bright leaves, and the birds built their nests.

One day Mrs Apple said, 'Rex will be here tomorrow.

95

Do you remember Rex? Of course you do. I'm sending Mother Broody's children to Rex's Missus. They are nearly grown up now, pullets in fact, and Rex is coming to help me catch them.'

Rex arrived on the early morning bus. Black Dog and Rex had not met before, so Tooty took the matter in hand. She took Black Dog to the gate to greet Rex.

'Good morning, Rex,' she said. 'This is my great friend,

Black Dog. (Be quiet, Black Dog, there's no need to growl like that.) He has come to live with us.'

'Good morning,' said Rex, taking no notice of the growls. 'How do you like the country? I'm a town dog myself.'

'Mind your own business –' began Black Dog fiercely ...

'Now Black Dog,' said Tooty, 'there really is no excuse to be such a snarly-yowl. Rex has been here before. He is a friend of ours.'

'Friend or not, he's bigger than me. I'm taking no risks,' replied Black Dog, rumbling loudly.

'Bigger or not, Sir,' said Rex, 'I know my place as a guest. Pleased to meet you.'

'Go on, Black Dog, stop that noise and wag your tail this minute,' said Tooty. So Black Dog sniffed Rex's nose, and both dogs wagged their tails.

'Now,' said Tooty, 'I think we had better go to the orchard and tell Mother Broody about the pullets.' So all three dogs trotted through the garden and squeezed under the gate into the orchard.

Mother Broody's nine nearly grown-up children rushed towards them shouting, 'Hello! Hello! have you come to

feed us? All those silly old hens are in the hen cub laying eggs. Mother Broody is on one of the nests and won't get off. They won't let us in there. Thelma thinks she's going to lay an egg in the grass over here. Come and look.'

'I'm not going to show them where I'm going to lay my egg.' said one of them, a smirking expression on her face. 'You're mean to tell them.' She pecked at her sisters and a great cackling and pecking began.

'Oh, let's leave them alone,' said Black Dog. 'They're a stupid lot.'

'Thelma, indeed,' said Rex, 'what a remarkably silly name for a hen.'

Tooty led the way towards the hen cub, away from the squabbling pullets. The hens were inside chatting to each other.

'It's time those children of yours were out in the world, Mother Broody,' said one. 'Very flighty they are. Always tearing about and cackling. Quite a nuisance they are becoming.'

'Move over, Mother Broody,' said another. 'Haven't you laid that egg yet? You can't sit there all day you know,' and she squeezed in beside Mother Broody and edged her off the nest.

Mother Broody got up and said 'Choooook' in a gentle voice. She went out through the little door and stretched her wings and said 'Chooooook' again. Then she saw the dogs. 'Oh, good morning, Black Dog and Tooty,' she said, 'and Rex as well. How nice to see you. Are you here on a visit?'

'No, Ma'am,' answered Rex, 'only until the afternoon bus. Mrs Apple is letting my Missus have your pullets, and we're taking them back on the bus with us.'

'Dear me,' said Mrs Broody, 'This is a little sudden. But it is time that they settled down. They've become very independent and rather greedy lately. Quite trying for us hens. Will they have an orchard to live in?'

Rex explained that as his Missus lived in the town there was no orchard. 'But we've wired off the end of the garden and put a nice wooden hen house in it,' he said. 'So they will have plenty of room to run and scratch about.'

Mother Broody felt quite contented when she heard this. 'I shouldn't care for them to go to one of those places where they are shut up all day,' she remarked. 'As long as they have somewhere to scratch about for worms they will be all right.'

Mrs Apple called, 'Lunch-time!' from the cottage door. The dogs said 'Good-bye for now,' to the hens, and ran up the garden.

After lunch Mrs Apple said, 'I must catch those pullets up now. Will you all come and help me?' So all the animals went to the orchard with her. Mrs Apple carried a roomy hamper, and a pannikin of corn. First she scattered corn in the hen cub, and when all the hens went inside to eat it she shut the little door. 'That'll keep them out of the way,' she said.

All the pullets were down in the far corner of the orchard, watching Thelma, who was pretending to lay an egg. When they saw Mrs Apple and all the animals coming they rushed towards them cackling 'Look! Look! They're coming to feed us. Leave that egg, Thelma, this is much more important!' Mrs Apple scattered corn and they all began pecking.

'Now, you animals,' said Mrs Apple. 'Spread out across the corner, and don't let any of them rush out. You, Black Dog, guard the hamper, and when I put them in see that they don't get out again. Ready?' She put the hamper by Black Dog and opened a little trap door in its lid, just big enough to put a pullet through. Then she made a grab at the nearest pullet, caught it and popped it in through the trap door. This surprised it a great deal and it cackled with

99

indignation. There was nothing it could do about it, as Black Dog was sitting on the lid. She grabbed three more in rapid succession and pushed them in as well.

Black Dog put his nose close to the wicker work, snuffled at them and said, 'Quiet, now. Don't make such a fuss. You're not going to market. You're going home with Rex.'

The last five pullets were not so easy to catch. George and Shoosh crept very quietly up on either side of one of

them, and George made terrible faces at it to attract its attention so that Mrs Apple was able to pick it up, and Tooty cornered one very cleverly behind Mother Broody's little house, but the last three were very tiresome indeed.

Mrs Apple became very hot and rather cross.

'Oh, drat these blessed things,' she cried, missing Thelma's tail by an inch. The cats became bored and strolled away about their own affairs, but Rex, Black Dog and Tooty did their very best to help. At last two more were caught and pushed into the hamper, leaving only Thelma. Once they nearly had her, but she flew straight up in the air over Mrs Apple's head. 'We'll have to run her,' said Mrs Apple. 'Come on, Rex, you are the quickest. Off you go.'

So Rex gave chase. Wherever Thelma ran, there was Rex behind her, twisting, turning and doubling back amongst the apple trees and grass tufts. At last, finding herself close to the hamper, Thelma gave in, and allowed Mrs Apple to pick her up. Mrs Apple held her gently, and smoothed the feathers of her neck and back. 'Now, you silly young thing,' she said. 'Calm down. You've got yourself into quite a state. Into the hamper, now, and settle down with your sisters.' She pushed Thelma gently through the little trap door and put the hamper in the shade of an apple tree.

'Farmer Parsloe will be here any time now,' she said, 'to carry it to the bus,' and she went indoors to rest and cool down. The dogs lay on the stones outside the cottage door.

By and by Farmer Parsloe came. He fetched the hamper from the orchard and called Rex.

'Good-bye, Rex,' said Mrs Apple. 'Thank you for your help. Your Missus will be on the bus, so you can all travel home together. We shall wave from the gate.'

So Farmer Parsloe, Rex and the hamper set off down the lane to the bus stop, and Mrs Apple and the Pekes stood at the gate to see them go. When they were out of sight Mrs Apple went indoors and put the kettle on, and she and the Pekes had a very comfortable tea together. Tooty sang her sugar song, and had an extra lump for being such a clever Peke.

Thelma laid her egg in the hamper on the way to the town. All the pullets settled down well in Rex's garden, where they were very happy. They became good sensible laying birds and soon Rex's Missus was wondering if next spring one of them would accept a clutch of eggs and raise a family of her own.

14

Cats and Birds

One bright and blowy morning Mrs Apple decided to do a big wash and air her bedding.

She carried her sheets to the wash-house to boil them in the copper.

The wash-house was a little stone building attached to the cottage. It had a mossy roof and a chimney. It got very steamy inside on wash-days, and bright green little ferns grew in the cracks in the walls. A family of snails lived behind the doorpost.

Mrs Apple filled the copper with water from the well, then she lit the fire under it.

The copper was a round cauldron, built round with bricks. It had a wooden lid, and there was a hole underneath for the fire, which warmed the water by heating the bottom of the cauldron.

George and Shoosh watched these preparations with interest.

'We'll get up on the roof by the chimney, George,' said Shoosh. 'It'll be warm from the fire and out of the wind. Good place to bird-watch from.' So up they climbed, by way of a lilac bush, and settled down side by side. George dozed and Shoosh sat still and looked.

Mrs Apple went indoors to fetch her feather bed. She tumbled it down the stairs. Then, tugging at it, she managed to get it out through the cottage door. 'Nothing like a bit of windy sunshine to freshen up the feathers,' she gasped.

The Pekes thought this great fun, and barked and jumped around her. Mrs Apple thumped the feather bed. Black Dog seized it with his teeth and shook. Feathers flew.

The sparrows and chaffinches collected them later to line their nests.

Tooty sang as loudly as she could, 'Ming dogs, Ping dogs! Bouncy dogs, Black Dog! Sunny day, Happy day! Come and play in the orchard.' And away went both Pekes, their tails flying and their furry feet hardly touching the ground.

'That's got rid of them,' said Mrs Apple, putting sheets in the copper to boil.

'Now that that's over,' said George, opening one eye,

'perhaps we shall have a bit of peace and see some birds.'

'*You* won't unless you keep awake a bit,' said Shoosh.

From her perch in the apple tree Mrs Blackbird watched George and Shoosh. 'Now, dears,' she said to her fledglings, 'you see those two furry animals by the chimney?'

'Yes, Mother,' they said.

'Well, you keep well away from them; they sometimes pounce. Always keep on the little twigs at the end of a branch and you'll be quite safe. They are too fat and heavy to follow you there. When you are big you can do what I am going to do now. Sit still, and watch.'

She flew down on to the grass where she was joined by Mr Blackbird.

'Cat drill, my dear?' he said. 'Very well. You begin.'

Mrs Blackbird gazed hard at the cats, her head on one side. Then she jabbed at the earth with her beak, to see if there was a worm about, and moved four hops nearer to the outhouse. Then she looked at the cats, and again pretended to look for a worm, hopping nearer as she did so. By this time both cats were staring at her, their whiskers pricking forwards. Mrs Blackbird repeated her performance. This time Shoosh moved from his sitting position into a crouch – the pounce position Mrs Blackbird called it. Mrs Blackbird hopped two hops sideways, away from Shoosh.

At that moment Mr Blackbird flew very fast indeed, diving at the roof of the outhouse. He skimmed the cats, missing the chimney by the breadth of a feather, and screamed at the top of his piercing voice: 'Skip! Skip! Skip! SKIP! SKIP! SKIP!' He then went and perched in the apple tree. George and Shoosh, who hadn't noticed he was anywhere near, jumped nearly out of their skins,

ducked their heads, and crouched down close to the tiles.

George said, 'Drat that bird. He made me jump. No manners, dangerous thing to do, might have made us fall off this roof.'

Shoosh said nothing. He tried hard to look as if he had never heard of a blackbird in his life. 'When in doubt, wash,' he murmured, trying to lick the middle of his back.

Mrs Blackbird flew back to the fledglings in the apple tree. They were laughing so much they could hardly hold on to their twigs. Mr Blackbird flew to the top of the tree and began a loud and joyful song to the glory of blackbirds and the confusion of cats.

By now Mrs Apple had washed and rinsed her sheets and hung them on the line where they billowed and flapped and looked as white and fresh as pear blossom.

'Cuckoo! Cuckoo! Cuckoo!' came the call across the garden. 'Drat that bird,' said Mrs Apple, 'fair drives you cuckoo.'

'Another joke for Browny,' said Shoosh to George. George said nothing, he was dozing again. 'Cuckoo! Cuckoo!' shouted the bird again and again.

After lunch Mrs Apple emptied the copper, raked out the fire and tidied up the wash house. Then she tidied herself, and sat down under the damson tree with her mending, the Pekes lying at her feet, until tea time. Then she took the sheets indoors, folded and ironed them. It was even harder to get the feather bed back into the house than it had been to get it out, but she managed.

In the evening the weather turned damp and a gentle drizzle began to fall. The cats took an evening stroll up the green lane leading to Farmer Parsloe's hayfield.

They put up with the rain because they were on the look-out for voles. They walked quietly, not talking at all, until they were underneath a crab-apple tree in full bloom. Here they stopped, and sat peering into the long grass. Suddenly, right over their heads they heard, 'kr : kr : kr :' (a kind of winding-up noise) then a very loud 'CUCKOO.'

'*Drat* that bird,' said George. 'He's very close indeed when you can hear him make that kr : kr : noise.'

Both cats sat peering up into the blossom.

'You know, we can't catch him,' said Shoosh. 'We can't

even see him amongst all these flowers. And he *always* flies away.' Sure enough the cuckoo wasn't there. 'Cuckoo,' came his voice, from the other side of the field.

The cats got up and turned homewards. They were silent and rather subdued.

But as they squeezed under the gate, 'Cuckoos are not good eating,' said George, and, 'He'll fly away altogether soon,' said Shoosh. And they made their way towards their own woodshed.

15

The Fight

One bright June morning Mrs Apple was sitting under the damson tree, shelling her early peas, with the Pekes lying at her feet, when in at the garden gate walked her neighbour, Farmer Parsloe, with his dog, Rags, at his heels. Rags looked a little embarrassed, because he and Black Dog had never become real friends. However, since his master said, 'Come along in, and keep to heel,' Rags did just that.

A long rumbling growl began, apparently somewhere near Black Dog's tail, and died away as Mrs Apple said, 'That's quite enough. Stop it, Black Dog.'

'Goodness me,' said Farmer Parsloe, looking at Black Dog. 'What is all the fuss about?' and he held his hand down for Black Dog to sniff at. Black Dog sniffed and wagged his tail. He got up and put his paws up on Farmer Parsloe's legs.

'That's quite a welcome,' said Mrs Apple. 'He's not like that with everyone.'

Black Dog rubbed his ears on Farmer Parsloe's hand. 'Not a breed I care for much,' said Farmer Parsloe, 'but I ...'

Tooty sprang to her feet and interrupted, 'That, Sir, is an insult!' she barked. 'We're Sing Dogs, Sung Dogs, Ming Dogs, Ping Dogs, and we come from Peking, and we're *Royal* – so there! – If you like him, Black Dog – I don't!'

And quite bristly with crossness she sat down with her
back to everybody.

But Black Dog went on nuzzling Farmer Parsloe's hand,
and chewed a ring he wore on his little finger.

Tooty growled.

'Tooty, that's not like you,' said Mrs Apple. 'You must
have got out of your basket on the wrong side this morning.'

'He's a great ignorant *man*!' said Tooty, 'and any
minute now I think he will tread on my tail.'

'Not if you wag it,' said Black Dog. He stopped chewing
the ring and looked round. 'Go on, Tooty,' he said. '*Wag*!
– Not everyone can know we are Palace Dogs from Peking
– W A G – or you may get stepped on!'

Farmer Parsloe held down his other hand. 'Come on now,' he said. 'Be friends.' Tooty got up, and sniffed at it, her neck stretched out as long as it would go, so that she didn't have to come too close.

Then she lifted up her head and her tail, and barked as loudly as ever she could, and began to prance – and with every prance she felt better tempered.

'I see the grass in your orchard is getting full long,' said Farmer Parsloe to Mrs Apple. 'Would you like Browny to come and gnaw it off a bit?'

'Indeed I would,' said Mrs Apple. 'Such a nice quiet old horse as ever I saw. He's friends with my animals, you know.'

'I'll bring him along this evening then,' said Farmer Parsloe. 'Come along, Rags. We'd best be getting back to work now. Good-day to you, Mrs Apple.' And with Rags close to his heel, he walked out of the gate, and Mrs Apple went into the cottage with her peas.

'Black Dog,' said Tooty. 'Why ever did you growl so horridly at Rags?'

'I think he's been at my bone-yard,' said Black Dog. 'I've lost a most valuable bone – just ripe for eating – been keeping it for a rainy day.'

'I don't think Rags can have taken it,' said Tooty. 'Your bone-yard is down by the gate to the hen field – I've never seen him come in here, except with Farmer Parsloe.'

'We'll see,' said Black Dog. 'When I catch him on neutral ground I think I'll nip him first, and ask afterwards.'

'You'll look a bit silly if it wasn't him,' said Tooty.

'My dear, you're a wise and pretty animal,' said Black Dog, 'but you must let us dogs manage such matters in our own way. You ladies don't understand.'

Mrs Apple came walking towards the gate. 'Come along, Pekes,' she called. 'Come and do the shopping with me.'

When they got to the shop, Mrs Apple opened the door. There was a bell fixed to it. It rang loudly: ting-a-ling.

Mrs Watson, whose shop it was, said, 'Good morning, Mrs Apple. What can I get for you?'

Mrs Apple said, 'Well, now, where's my list? Oh yes. A pound of candles, please, half a pound of best tea, a quarter of tangerine drops. And can you let me have a bit of meal for the hens? Mine's late coming this week.'

Mrs Watson had just opened her mouth to say, 'Oh yes, I can manage that,' when in walked Farmer Parsloe with Rags. Black Dog was on his feet in a second. He walked up to Rags on very stiff legs, and said, loud and clear, 'DOG, I have lost a most valuable bone, and have reason to believe you've had it.'

'ANIMAL, I have not,' said Rags even louder and clearer.

'Well, if you haven't, someone has,' said Black Dog. 'And I'd like a fight! ANIMAL YOURSELF!'

'Oh, you would, would you, you black lump of fur,' said Rags – and in a flash they were rolling all over the floor, bouncing into biscuit tins and making terrible growling and snarling noises. Mrs Apple joined Mrs Watson behind the counter. Farmer Parsloe shouted and whacked about with his stick. Tooty became quite frantic and barked and barked.

Black Dog nipped Rags in the back leg. Rags caught hold of Black Dog by his thick ruff and shook him. Mrs Watson threw a handful of tangerine drops at them. The tangerine drops were sticky, and stuck in the fur of both dogs. Tooty lay on her back on the floor and screamed.

Rags let go of Black Dog in surprise, and looked at Tooty. Farmer Parsloe grabbed Black Dog and put him on the counter, from which height Black Dog could look down on Rags. Both dogs looked delighted with themselves.

Mrs Apple came out from behind the counter and gave Tooty a sharp slap. Then Farmer Parsloe picked her up and rubbed her behind her ears until she felt better. 'There, there, my dear. It's all over now,' he said. 'And by the look of them, they enjoyed their scrap. Come on now, you two dogs. Friends now?' So Black Dog and Rags wagged their tails and sniffed noses.

'Did you have that bone?' asked Black Dog.

'No,' said Rags, 'I didn't.'

'Oh well, never mind,' said Black Dog. 'I enjoyed that fight, did you?' And they trotted off, leading the way home.

Farmer Parsloe went to collect Browny the horse from his field, to take him to Mrs Apple's orchard.

They all walked up to the cottage together, and were met at the gate by the cats.

'Hello,' said Shoosh, 'we missed you. Had a good walk?'

'I think it's tea-time,' said George. So they all had tea together under the damson tree.

It turned out that Mother Broody had scratched up the bone, when digging worms for her children. She didn't mention the matter because she didn't realize the bone was valuable.

However, Black Dog and Rags became firm friends, and there were never any more misunderstandings.

16

Mrs Apple's Birthday

One fine morning the cats, George and Shoosh, woke up before the sun. They were arranging their whiskers under the damson tree when the first rays shone on them.

'Going to be warm today,' said George. 'I have a feeling that there may be something special about today, but I forget what it is.' Shoosh got up and stretched his front legs out as far as they would go and yawned. He couldn't remember either. He stared fixedly at Mrs Blackbird up in the damson tree, who stared back. 'Not knowing, can't say,' he replied.

Inside the cottage the sun shone through a crack in the curtains on to Black Dog, curled up asleep in his basket. He woke, and trotted to the door. He snuffled under it. 'Come on Toots,' he said. 'Time to wake up. I feel it in my blood and bones that today isn't an ordinary day. It is different.'

Tooty looked at him over the edge of her basket. 'Let's wake Mrs Apple,' she said. So both Pekes barked until Mrs Apple's door opened and she came downstairs. She looked rather sleepy.

'Pekes,' she said, 'it's very early, but it is a special day. Trust you animals to know. My birthday, too.' She opened the door and out bounded the Pekes.

'Hello, cats!' barked Black Dog. 'It is a special day. Mrs Apple said so. Did you know?'

'Of course,' said both cats, at once – you can never catch a good cat napping.

'Well, what then?' asked Black Dog. 'Tooty and I don't know what is special about it.' But the cats pretended not to hear.

Mrs Apple brought breakfast out of doors under the damson tree. Cornflakes and cream for everybody. Mrs Apple threw some cornflakes to Mrs Blackbird.

After breakfast Mrs Apple said, 'I'm going indoors to ice a cake. Rex is coming this afternoon, and we are going to have my birthday party in the fields with Browny and Farmer Parsloe. We'll be out rather late, because today is today,' and she disappeared into the cottage.

'What *is* today?' asked Tooty. 'None of us know. Let's go and ask the cows.' So all four animals went through the orchard where the hens live, past Mother Broody, who was sitting in her little house with her new, very tiny, chicks. 'Where are you off to?' she asked, poking her head out through the slats of the front of her coop.

'It's a special day,' answered Tooty. 'But we don't know why. So we're going to ask the cows.'

'I believe I know,' said Mother Broody. 'It feels special to me too.'

The cows had just got back to their field after morning milking. 'Lovely day for the time of year,' they said, and gazed at the four animals.

'What's special about today?' asked Black Dog.

'Time of year,' said a big black and white cow gazing at a buttercup. 'Comes only once, like Christmas,' said another, staring away over the field, and chewing. 'Time of year,' mooed several cows together, 'Time of year.'

Black Dog looked mystified. 'Whatever do they mean?' he asked.

'Black Dog!' exclaimed Tooty suddenly. 'I understand! Once a year, like Christmas. It's Midsummer Day! the special day for fairies and magic. Cows know all about that. There's a fairy called Robin Goodfellow who looks after cows. He keeps away the bad magic which turns their milk sour.'

'Of *course*,' said Black Dog. 'I remember when I lived with the gipsies they tied the horse up very carefully on Midsummer Night, in case he went away with the fairies. They used to shut their caravans up extra carefully too, in case the fairies took a fancy to one of their babies and gave them a fairy child in exchange. No wonder we're going to have a picnic. I wonder where we're going?'

Mrs Apple came out of the cottage. 'Rex is here,' she said. 'Come and have lunch. Then, when Farmer Parsloe arrives we'll set off.'

All the animals knew Rex, who had visited End Cottage before, and were glad to see him. The day had become so warm that they all had lunch under the damson tree.

'Do you know what day it is?' asked Tooty.

'Yes. Mrs Apple's birthday,' answered Rex.

'Midsummer Day, as well. Fairies and such like, you know,' said Black Dog, looking up from his food bowl.

'Fairies are rot,' said Rex briefly.

'Oh, Rex! ...' began Tooty, really shocked.

'Only a town dog could say a thing like that,' interrupted Black Dog. 'I thought so once myself. Now I know better.'

'Don't gobble so, or you'll choke,' said Mrs Apple.

After lunch everyone found their favourite place for a nap. George went to his clump of thyme, Black Dog and Tooty went to their baskets, and Rex stayed with Mrs Apple under the damson tree. Shoosh disappeared. He didn't have a nap, but heavy thumps, scutterings, and rat-like squeaks were heard from the woodshed during the afternoon.

At about five o'clock Mrs Apple went into the cottage. She came out again carrying the picnic basket and a rug.

'Come along,' she said. 'Farmer Parsloe will be here in a minute with Browny and the cart.'

Rex and the Pekes led the way to the gate. 'Come along, cats,' called Mrs Apple, and George and Shoosh walked up the path, purring and waving their tails.

'Shall we walk or ride?' said Shoosh.

'I shall ride,' said George, 'it's not every day that a cat gets a chance to ride in a cart.'

Just then Farmer Parsloe's voice said 'Whoa, Browny,' and the cart stopped at the gate.

'Many happy returns of the day, Mrs Apple,' he said. 'Get in everybody. I haven't brought Rags with me. He has stayed to look after the cows.'

Mrs Apple lifted the Pekes into the back of the cart, and climbed up beside Farmer Parsloe. The cats leapt in with graceful bounds, and Rex scrambled in at the back.

'Hold on,' said Browny. 'I'm going to start,' and clickety-clop, rumble-rumble, away they went. The lane stretched before them, flowery verges and hedges bright with dog roses on each side. The cows watched from the fields. 'Happy Birthday,' they mooed, and Mrs Apple waved to them.

Soon Browny turned in at an open gate, and took them up a slope under some nut trees. The track was quite steep. 'This is far enough to pull the cart,' said Browny. 'Take me out of the shafts, and we'll walk the last bit.'

So Farmer Parsloe unharnessed him, while Mrs Apple lifted the Pekes down. 'Oh, a lovely place,' they barked. 'Bouncy dogs. Happy dogs,' and they rushed up the track with Rex behind them.

The cats followed, and Mrs Apple and Farmer Parsloe

walked behind carrying the picnic basket and a rug. The leafy branches of the nut trees met over their heads, so that they walked through a tunnel, where the light was dusky green. When they came out at the end into dazzling sunshine Mrs Apple stopped and looked about her, at a wide sloping field which ran down to the edge of a big pond, and up over the brow of a little hill. 'What a lovely place,' she said. 'Let's carry our basket nearer to the pond, then we'll have our picnic.'

The Pekes and Rex ran on ahead, and found a smooth grassy place, close to the water. Here Mrs Apple spread the rug. The Pekes bounded down to the pond and Rex made a great leap and landed with a splash about a yard from the edge. He swam strongly out to the middle, then turned and swam back. 'Absolutely splendid!' he barked, coming ashore and shaking off showers of spray.

'Mind the picnic, you great wet thing!' exclaimed Mrs Apple.

The Pekes rushed about barking. Then Tooty, feeling hot, lay on her tummy in the shallows, and Black Dog stood up to his waist in water and lapped.

'A fine mess you dogs have made of yourselves,' said Mrs Apple. 'Lucky there's plenty of grass to rub dry on.'

'Come, now,' said Farmer Parsloe. 'Shall we unpack the picnic? I want to see the cake.'

'Here it is,' said Mrs Apple, lifting it out of her basket. It was a fine big one with pink icing, and A. Apple written on it with little bits of cherries. They arranged it on a white cloth on the grass. It looked quite beautiful. Browny stopped grazing and walked over to admire it. The cats had appeared, and everybody sat down in a circle and the picnic began. There was jelly and strawberries as well as

the cake. Mrs Apple and Farmer Parsloe had tea out of a thermos. Tooty and the cats drank milk. Rex and Black Dog refused milk, being full of pond water.

After tea Mrs Apple and Farmer Parsloe played lazy games like 'I Spy with my little eye something beginning with ...' and when it was B and it was Browny, it wasn't fair because Browny had walked away out of sight. The animals lay quietly chatting, digesting cake.

By and by it began to be dusk. The cats sat staring about them with brilliant eyes. The Pekes lay with their noses on their paws, ears forward, listening, bright eyes watching. 'What's that?' said Tooty quickly. At the same moment Black Dog gave a little whickering growl.

Rex looked at them. 'You two are seeing things,' he said, and rolled on the grass.

The cats said nothing. They went on staring into the

dusk with shining eyes. Browny came trotting over the brow of the hill. He stopped, looked over his shoulder and whinnied gently. Wild roses were twisted in his mane. He stood listening, his head held high.

The cats got up and walked over the grass towards Browny. Soon they began to run. The Pekes jumped up and followed, Black Dog running with his nose to the ground, Tooty just behind him. Browny kicked up his heels and galloped away. The cats and the Pekes ran faster, and faster, and faster, and they all swept over the curve of the land and disappeared.

Rex stopped rolling and rushed to Mrs Apple.

'Careful, you great muddy thing,' she said. 'I do believe you must have got fleas, the way you go on.'

Farmer Parsloe looked at him and shook his head. 'I don't think it's fleas,' he said. 'I believe he's frightened.'

Mrs Apple glanced over her shoulder rather uneasily. 'I think we ought to be getting back home,' she said. 'Where have they all got to?' So she and Farmer Parsloe stood up and called all the animals by name, Rex keeping close to their heels.

The animals came quietly out of the dusk. It was as if they had never been away. Browny's roses had gone, but one pink petal clung to Black Dog's ruff.

Farmer Parsloe picked up the picnic basket, and they walked into the nut tunnel. It was nearly dark under the branches.

The Pekes trotted along quietly, side by side.

'Only once a year,' said Black Dog.

'Yes,' said Tooty. She sounded a little sad.

Browny had reached the cart and Farmer Parsloe was putting him into the shafts. Rex said, loudly and defiantly,

'I *said* fairies are rot.' Then he leapt into the cart and hid under the seat.

'You're stupid,' said Black Dog. And the cats, coming from the shadows of the hedge, grinned. Their eyes still shone, but now they were thinking of mice.

When everyone was comfortably settled in the cart, Browny said: 'Off I go,' and away they went, trit-trot, clippety-clop, rumble-rumble, along the lane towards home.

Soon the moon rose over the fields and Tooty began to sing.

'Sing-a-song of happy days, birthday dogs, summer dogs,
Sing-a-song for Black Dog, George and Shoosh.
Sing for little Tooty-Pooty, (very full of birthday cake,)
Sleepy dog, happy dog, . . .

and her voice drifted away in a little babble, as she fell asleep beside Black Dog.

By and by Browny stopped outside the End Cottage, and the birthday was over.

Also in Young Puffin

THE RAILWAY CAT

Phyllis Arkle

Railway Porter v. Railway Cat. Who will win?

Alfie the railway cat lives at the station where he's a favourite with all the regular passengers. The only trouble is that Hack, the new railway porter, doesn't like cats and he soon has a plan for getting rid of Alfie.

Also in Young Puffin

THE RAILWAY CAT AND DIGBY

Phyllis Arkle

Alfie the railway cat is in trouble again!

Somehow Alfie always seems to be in Leading Railman Hack's bad books. He tries very hard to make friends with Hack, but with little success. And when Alfie decides to try and improve matters by 'helping' Hack's dog, Digby, win a prize at the local show, things rapidly go from bad to worse!

OLGA
Takes Charge

Michael Bond

Graham was in love. There was no doubt about it.

Olga da Polga cannot believe that her friend Graham the tortoise has fallen for someone who doesn't speak and who is so tall that he cannot even see her eyes. With her usual sense of 'sorting things out', Olga sets out to discover what's really going on in the garden.